"May, are you upset with me?"

"Why should there be something wrong?" she huffed.

"Why does your tone say differently?" Thad tried to search her eyes.

"Listen, Thad." May's voice lowered to a controlled tone. "You made a fool of me once before. You're not going to do it again. I'm moving to Indiana. I suggest you have someone else care for Leah."

He took a couple steps backward. "May, I'm not seeing anyone."

She shook her head. "Your personal life is none of my business. I'll watch Leah until you can find someone else. I'll see you tomorrow." She closed the kitchen door and that was that.

Stunned, Thad stared at the door. He carried Leah down the porch steps to the buggy and set her bassinet on the seat. It was his fault trying to rekindle their relationship. There would always be that doubt in May's heart. He'd never be able to convince her that he did care for her. That he had always cared for her…

Marie E. Bast grew up on a farm in northern Illinois. In the solitude of country life, she often read or made up stories. She earned a BA, an MBA and an MA in general theology and enjoyed a career with the federal government, but characters kept whispering her name. She retired and now pursues her passion of full-time writing. Marie loves walking, golfing with her husband of twenty-seven years and baking. Visit Marie at mariebast.Blogspot.com.

Books by Marie E. Bast

Love Inspired

The Amish Baker
The Amish Marriage Bargain

Visit the Author Profile page at Harlequin.com.

The Amish
Marriage Bargain

Marie E. Bast

Recycling programs
for this product may
not exist in your area.

 LOVE INSPIRED BOOKS

ISBN-13: 978-1-335-42936-0

The Amish Marriage Bargain

Copyright © 2019 by Marie Elizabeth Bast

www.Harlequin.com

Printed in U.S.A.

But if ye forgive not men their trespasses,
neither will your Father forgive your trespasses.
—*Matthew* 6:15

To past and present dairy farmers in my life: my husband, Darrell; brothers Robert and Richard; and my extended family, Jesus Návar.

In loving memory of Michael, my brother, and Richard Walline, my father, who wisely raised me on a milking farm—one of the best times of my life. I love you both dearly and miss you.

To the Iowa Amish organic dairy farmers, and all farmers who work hard from sunrise to sunset and beyond.

Also, to Melissa, my superhero editor, who has a keen eye, a fierce red pen and spot-on guidance; the Harlequin publishing team (my white knights); and Scribes202: Laura H., Linda M., Linda H., Heidi, Christy, Kathy and Julie. I love you all.

And to Cyle Young, my agent, who gives subtle, awe-inspiring nuggets of advice.

Last, but certainly not least, Kayla Caudle, who mentioned she lived by a dairy farm…

Chapter One

Washington County, Iowa

May Bender had made her decision, but how could she possibly tell him?

Conjuring up the strength of a Goliath, she readied herself for battle. But first, she set dinner on the table, lifted her year-old niece, Leah, into her high chair and handed her a piece of bread smeared with jelly. Leah tilted her head and gifted *aentie* with a very toothy smile.

She was going to miss this little pumpkin. May wrestled a tear from her cheek with the tip of her finger.

Tucking that sad thought away, she eased onto the chair across the table from Thad and bowed her head for silent prayer. After the blessing, she took potatoes for her and Leah's plate, then handed the bowl to Thad. His hand glided over hers as he grabbed the bowl. She jerked her hand back as a tingle shot up her arm.

Thad, toting a farmer's appetite, loaded his plate and took a bite of pork chop. "Mmm, *gut*."

The compliment stunned her. He didn't often hand them out. In fact, they didn't often talk much at all. "*Danki*, it was just a little seasoning. That reminds me, the door on the spice cupboard sticks and a couple of the others are swollen from humidity."

Without raising his head, Thad nodded. "I'll take care of them on the next rainy day."

May took a slice of bread, buttered it and pushed a few crumbs off the table, watching them drop to the floor like pieces of her life. Her faith taught her to forgive, but how could she forget April and Thad's betrayal when he sat across the table from her every day?

. Leah picked up a few peas with her index finger and thumb. Dropping a couple, she managed to shove a few in her mouth, giggling at her achievement. She smacked her lips and handed her soggy bread to *Aent* May. *"Mamm, Mamm, Mamm..."*

"Oh, *danki* for sharing, but you can keep it, sweetie."

Pushing her hand in her pocket, May touched the letter, to draw encouragement. "Thad, my *aent* in Indiana has offered me a job. She wants me to help run her café and bake shop in Shipshewana and take it over when she retires. Edna has given me three months to make up my mind."

He took another bite of food but didn't respond.

May didn't need twelve weeks to think it over; she just needed to box up all her belongings and make the arrangements. It was time she moved. Time she got away from Thad Hochstetler, her brother-in-law. A man who had once courted May, then dumped her for her beautiful sister, April.

She raised her chin to face him. "You know you'll need to hire a nanny?"

He took another bite of pork chop, then nodded.

May glared at him. Nineteen months ago, Thad had brought May home from singings, and April rode with his *bruder* Alvin. Her sister must have loved Alvin. They had both been baptized, joined the church and their banns were set to be read on the next Church Sunday. Six weeks after Alvin's death from his buggy accident, April and Thad wed.

Thad cleared his throat. Deep lines creased his forehead just under a dark brown swatch of hair that had fallen forward. He raised his head and locked eyes with hers. His mouth twisted into a weak smile, the edges nervously twitching. "Would you…consider postponing your plan to move to Indiana? I hate to ask this, but I'd appreciate it if you would stay on a little while longer and watch Leah."

"What?" A tear pressed at the corner of her eye. "You're joking, right?"

"The farm's income has declined by almost 35 percent this past year with the problem The Amish Dairy Association has been having with the USDA and its inspection agencies. Small farmers are losing money by the day trying to compete with the big dairy producers out west when they violate the organic rules and overproduce." His voice quaked. "The inspection agencies have been lax in suspending violators and writing citations for fines. I can't afford a full-time nanny right now with a mortgage, and *Mamm*'s arthritic hips won't allow her to chase a one-year-old all day."

May drew a deep breath, holding it deep in her chest before blowing it out. "The longer I postpone the move, the harder it will be on Leah." *And me.*

"Look, May, I'm in dire straits here… I could lose the farm."

Contempt for him boiled her blood. "You mean my *mamm* and *daed*'s farm that you inherited from my sister. It's been in our family for 170 years." She spit out the words as if they were wrapped with barbed wire.

"Small dairy farmers are being driven out of business all over the Midwest." He let his gaze drop, then raised his eyes to meet her glare. "I'd really appreciate it if you could stay a while longer."

May fisted her hands. Her world was tumbling, as if a spool of thread dropped to the floor, unraveling before her eyes.

She heaved a sigh but caught the look of pleading cross his face, then vanish in a heartbeat. "I'll think about it."

Thad nodded, scooted his chair away from the table, snatched his straw hat from the peg on the wall, plopped it on and headed outside.

May clutched her chest while pain arrowed through her. Why had she told him she'd think about it? She had thought about it, and the time was right to move.

She dropped her fork and covered her face with her hands. *Nein. Nein. Nein.*

April's words whirled through her head. *"I'm dying, sister. Promise me you'll take care of Leah and Thad."*

"Nein, April, I can't do that. Not after what Thad did..."

"I feel the life draining from me. You must do it, May, please! Forgive me. Thad and I never meant to hurt you. Things just happen." April exhaled a long breath and closed her eyes. Her hand fell limp.

May steered her mind back to the present.

Why had she made that promise?

A blast of evening air squeezed through the screen in the door and circulated around the room, giving it a fresh scent. While Leah played on the floor with her blocks, May stowed her decision for now, washed the dishes and straightened the kitchen.

When Leah started to fuss and rub her

eyes, May snatched her up and snuggled her close. "I won't be able to do this much longer if I decide to go, little one." She kissed Leah's sweet little head when she laid it against her shoulder, almost falling asleep. "*Nein*, let's get you bathed and settled in bed."

After putting the child to sleep, May closed Leah's door with Thad's request still whirling in her head. How could she stay here? He was certainly insensitive to her need. Her fingers twitched with the impulse to start packing now. She'd never be able to sleep. Tiptoeing quietly down the hall, she headed to her sewing room.

Sewing always calmed her nerves.

She grabbed her basket of long strips of cloth she'd torn from old clothes and started sewing them together to make rag rugs. She finished connecting the last strips together, then glanced at the battery clock. *Ach*. Midnight. After tidying the sewing room, she trudged down the hall to her room and collapsed on her bed.

She rubbed her hand over her quilt. The softness of the cottton reminded her of Leah when she was born. Her sweet *boppli* softness, and even then, she was as lovely as April with dark blue eyes like Thad's. She'd hated her sister for stealing Thad from her, but how could she stay angry when April was dead? She would have been so proud of her *tochter.*

Oh, April, you were so careless in caring for yourself and letting the diabetes get out of control, like it had with Mamm.

May pressed her hand over her eyes to blot out all the ugliness she'd silently heaped upon April.

Lord, please forgive me for my sins. It was sisterly rivalry, or maybe jealousy that I coveted what she had. April always got what she wanted, and I got her hand-me-downs. Thad had a right to choose, and he chose April. I can't even tell her I'm sorry. Your scripture says I must forgive, but it's hard to forget the trespass. Help me to learn.

A deep yawn coaxed her out of her shoes. She removed her prayer *kapp*, letting her long auburn hair cascade over her shoulders. After putting on her nightgown, she burrowed under the covers, drowsiness tugging at her eyes.

She loved Leah so much, but she couldn't pass up the opportunity that *Aent* Edna offered. Could she? A once-in-a-lifetime offer?

Could she pass it up to help Thad? For the sake of the farm?

But Edna's offer was a vote to move.

The next morning, sunshine poured in between the curtains and roused May from sleep. She glanced at the clock. *Ach*, 7:00 a.m. The thought of Thad waiting in the kitchen hungry pushed the cloudiness from her head. A *gut* Amish woman always saw to it that the men had a nourishing meal before they started their workday.

Although *Daed* assured May she could stay in the *haus* until she married, it was uncomfortable living with Thad. That was another vote in favor of moving.

She dressed and hurried downstairs. When she entered the kitchen, the aroma of strong coffee assaulted her nose. Thad stood over the stove, bacon in one pan and French toast in another. Her eyes roamed from the stove to Leah in her high chair, smiling as she ate scrambled eggs. She held her little hand out and offered May a gob of egg.

"*Danki, lieb,* but you eat it." She turned to Thad. "I'm so sorry I overslept. I don't know what got into me." Something she never wanted to have to do…apologize to Thad Hochstetler.

He turned and swept his arm in the direction of the table. "Sit. Your breakfast awaits you, Miss Bender."

He was being nice, too nice. Now what did he want?

Thad smiled. "I noticed you worked late in your sewing room. We're a family and that means we help each other out. Occasionally, we forget to set our alarms. No harm done. Sit. Breakfast is ready." He placed the platter on the table and sat.

After silent prayer, May dribbled syrup on her French toast and took a bite.

He scooted a slice onto his plate and ladled strawberries over top. "Mmm, your garden strawberries are *gut*. I picked them fresh this morning."

May tossed him a she-could-hardly-believe-it stare.

A knock on the door pierced the silence, then the screen door popped open. Lois Plank, the midwife, and her son Elmer stepped in.

"*Hullo.* Come in and sit." Thad motioned with his free hand.

"It smells *gut* in here." Elmer stuck his nose in the air and took a couple of deep whiffs. "Only it's a little late for breakfast."

Lois raised a brow at Elmer's nosy remark. "I'm sorry to interrupt, but I've come to give Leah her twelve-month checkup."

"Of course!" May stood and pulled Leah out of her high chair. Lois followed May into the other room.

"How's the cheese business, Elmer?" Thad leaned back in his chair and glanced at his guest. "Looks like you dashed over here right from your factory."

Elmer brushed a hand down the front of his shirt. "*Jah, Mamm* doesn't like to drive all over the township by herself when she makes her rounds."

Thad listened to Elmer drone on, naming all the other homes they would visit today. When the women returned to the kitchen, May sat Leah in the middle of the floor with her toys.

"Lois, Elmer, would you like a cup of coffee?" May grabbed the pot off the stove and placed it on the hotplate as she sat. "Please sit."

"*Nein.* I have other appointments. We need to get going." Lois motioned for Elmer to head for the door, which he ignored.

Thad cut into another piece of French

toast, put it in his mouth and watched Elmer scurry to May's side, slipping into the chair next to hers.

Thad sniffed and breathed in a tangy whiff of cheese stuck to Elmer's shirt. The smear of ripened cheddar from Elmer's aging room seemed to mingle with his blue cheese spot. Thad stifled a smile. Elmer called himself a cheese artisan.

"How are you, May?" Elmer's voice dripped with concern. He leaned toward May, put his arm around the back of her chair and pressed in closer. "I'll stop by tomorrow." He tossed Thad a better-not-try-to-stop-me look, quickly adding, "Thad, are you attending the meeting tonight over at the Millers' dairy on the USDA's organic standard?"

"Wouldn't miss it." Thad glared at the cheesemaker. He wanted to tell Elmer to stay away from May, but she'd resent his interference.

Elmer leaned even closer to May. "I noticed your garden has a lot of beans ready to harvest, and you'll probably want them for your vegetable stand. Why don't I stop back later and help you pick them? It'll be cooler this evening."

"*Danki*, Elmer, but aren't you going to the meeting?"

"I'll go late. They chew over everything before they get down to business." Elmer threw Thad a sly smile.

"Are you sure you don't want a cup of coffee?" May started to stand.

Lois shook her head. "*Danki*, we need to go if we're going to stick to our schedule. Elmer, it's time."

The screen door squeaked open and the distinctive shuffle that followed pulled Thad to his feet. "*Gut* mornin', *Mamm*." His cheeks burned as he caught a hint of judgment in her eyes.

"What's going on in here?" Gretchen took a deep breath and looked around. "Are you still lollygagging over breakfast? You should be out in the field, *jah*?" She tossed a sour glance at Thad, then turned toward the table with a stern look. "May, you need to get up earlier and get the food on the table by five thirty. April never ran her *haus* like this. There are beans in the garden to be picked and canning that needs to be done."

Elmer stood and gave a nod. "*Gut* mornin', Gretchen. Nice to see you. I forgot you and Aaron were staying in Thad's *dawdi haus* while the one on Jonah's farm was being refurbished."

"It's nice to see you, too, Elmer. Lois, you checking on our Leah?"

"Indeed. She's a sweet little thing and in *gut* health. No worry with her, Gretchen. May, don't forget about the quilting frolic in three weeks."

"*Jah*, it's on my calendar."

Elmer held the screen door for his *mamm*. "See you later, May."

Thad pulled his hat from the peg on the wall and headed out the door with a sideways glance at May. She sent him a glare.

He'd hurt May when he'd tossed her

aside for her sister. There was no way to apologize for that but his sharp-tongued *mamm* only made things worse. "Come on, *Mamm*, I'll walk you out."

In the evening, May and Leah sat on the porch and watched Thad disappear into the barn after he'd hitched Tidbit to the buggy. Twenty minutes passed. Her gaze swung from the barn door to Tidbit as he pawed the ground nervously, waiting to stretch his legs. Why was Thad taking so long getting ready to go to the dairy association meeting?

A buggy turned into the driveway, the wheels crunching over the rocks as she watched Elmer park it in front of the *haus*. He stepped down and waved as he walked toward her.

Elmer was handsome and his bronzed skin set off his sky blue eyes. He'd definitely be a *gut* catch for some woman, but not her. She only thought of him as a friend, and he deserved a *frau* that would *liebe* him.

Thad closed the barn door and stalked toward the *haus*, a grimace plastered on his face as he nodded to Elmer. Ah, now she understood why Thad had stalled after hitching Tidbit. *Elmer.*

When they were all *kinner* in school, Thad and Elmer had some kind of rivalry. It seemed like everything was a competition to them, horseback riding, swimming, but it was more than that. But she couldn't quite tag it. If she didn't know better, she'd think Thad was jealous. *Nein*, that couldn't be. It was just their old silliness, like two small *buwe.*

A smile tugged at her lips as Elmer got closer. He had donned a clean blue chambray shirt and trousers. *Gut.* He had smelled like cheese curds earlier in the day.

Before Elmer reached the steps, Thad smacked the reins across Tidbit's back, and the buggy shot off down the driveway toward the gate. May gripped her apron as she watched the speeding buggy. She relaxed as Tidbit slowed before he crossed the road.

"*Gut* evening, May. How are you this evening?"

"A bit tired."

"*Jah?* I'll stay only a little while."

She faced Elmer, then glanced at the road after Thad. A twinge of sadness washed over her. She couldn't believe that Thad might lose the farm. Her family's farm. *Daed* and *Mamm* fought hard for years to keep the farm, to make the payments and to put food on the table every day. This land ran through her veins almost as much as her blood did. It was who she was. Even if she had to go door-to-door in town with a bucket of vegetables to make a sale, she'd do it.

Her heart pounded. That was a bad sign. Why was it that the mere sight of Thad made it hard for her to breathe? To walk in a straight line? And when his hand touched hers when she handed him the potato bowl, she nearly melted on the spot.

Jah, she either had to hide her heart or convince the angel Gabriel to protect it, or Thad would steal it away. *Nein*, not again! She didn't know what was worse…losing the farm or losing her heart.

But could she risk sticking around to find out?

Chapter Two

The next morning, Thad ran his hands through his hair as he entered the kitchen. "Mmm, sausage and eggs smell *gut*."

"Thought it was my turn to treat you to breakfast this morning," she turned and faced him. "How'd the dairy association meeting go last night?"

He pulled a chair away from the kitchen table and plopped down. "It doesn't look like the USDA is in any big hurry to make changes. That means that many farmers are going to have to sell organic for the regular milk price. We'll lose money, about 33 percent, by doing that, but it can't be helped."

"I'm sorry to hear that. I know how hard you work."

"*Jah*, well, times are changing."

"Maybe you could sell the cows and put in all produce?"

"The reason why we diversify is because a storm could wipe out the whole crop. This way we still have milk money to fall back on. The president of the association called the newspaper and a reporter showed up. He was going to put a story in the paper. Maybe the *Englisch* politicians will take notice. I'm praying for that."

May flashed him a hopeful smile.

"How's Leah? When I'm outside, I don't see her much. She's not up yet?"

"She was up earlier playing and had her breakfast. Now she's napping. We were outside all yesterday afternoon. She missed her nap, and went to bed early. It threw her off schedule."

"How is your vegetable stand doing?"

"It's doing very well. Lots of *Englisch* stop by the roadside stand wanting to buy fresh produce."

"Ah, *gut*. At least there is something we grow that the consumers like to buy."

They hadn't talked this much since they'd courted. Yet, if he was going to persuade her to stay, they'd need to be getting along a whole lot better. She set the breakfast on the table and sat opposite Thad. After the blessing, she poured his coffee and dished up her plate.

She only tolerated him, but in all fairness, he had dumped her and married her sister. He truly regretted that.

They both wanted the farm to succeed. And he sure hoped her *liebe* for it and Leah made her come to the right conclusion. But he needed to know where he stood with May.

A flash of fear tugged at his gut as he aimed his gaze across the table. "Have you made a decision yet about leaving Iowa?"

She raised her head and he could read the surprise on her face.

The words popped out before he could bite them back. He knew he shouldn't rush her. She needed time. He'd only push her into making a hasty decision. That probably wouldn't be in his favor.

"*Nein*. I'm taking my time—a move to Indiana is final. It's a big decision, and I want to get it right."

A sigh whooshed out before he could stop it. That meant he still had time to sway her decision.

But how could he convince her to stay?

May lugged the baskets of tomatoes and bins of green beans and peapods to her roadside stand she had put at the end of the driveway by the white fence. She arranged the quart-size cartons of strawberries in rows, then sat the plastic bags and cash box on the opposite end of the table.

She blotted her forehead with her hand as she glanced at the blanket on the ground where Leah sat playing. Her pumpkin was the only sweetness in her life. For sure and for certain, she was going to miss that little bit of sugar if she headed to Indiana. She'd told Thad she hadn't made a decision, but in truth, it was for the best that she moved. But she needed to consider it from all angles.

Someday Thad would want to remarry, and that would make it uncomfortable for her. Edna's offer was only for a short while, and she needed to take advantage of her generosity.

A warm breeze danced across her face, drying the perspiration on her forehead. She turned in that direction, stood for a minute and fully enjoyed the blessing.

It reminded her of the times she and April had sat under a tree one summer and talked about *buwe*. Who was the cutest, which one had the best personality, and who owned the broadest shoulders? Thad and Alvin tied for the win in all categories. A few pangs of homesickness stirred in her, knowing these would be her last few weeks on the land if she decided to move.

May glanced toward the barn where Thad stood looking her way. It was hard even imagining losing the family's farm.

She finished arranging her vegetable stand, then took a step back and glanced at the display in front of the white fence. Perfect.

She'd miss her garden and the stand, but surely *Aent* Edna had a patch behind her café and bake shop.

She picked up Leah and the blanket she was sitting and crawling on. Leah smiled so sweetly that it stole May's heart as she swung the tyke around. Leah giggled while little wisps of taffy-colored hair bounced around her cherub face. "*Mamm*, more!"

"*Nein*, it's time for your nap, little one."

"*Mamm*," Leah laughed.

May reached the porch and laid the blanket on a chair. She turned when she heard wheels rumbling into the drive.

Bishop Yoder climbed out of his buggy

and walked a few steps in her direction. "*Gut* afternoon, May. Another hot July day, *jah*? Is Thad around?"

"I believe he's in the shed boxing vegetables, Bishop. Would you like a glass of lemonade?"

He looked toward the shed, then back at May. "That does sound *gut*. Just a small one."

He followed her into the kitchen and plunked down on a chair waving his hat across his face.

"Would you rather sit on the porch?"

"*Nein*. This is fine."

She sat Leah on the floor by her toys, cut a piece of banana bread, poured a glass of lemonade and set them in front of him.

He took a bite of bread, then washed it down with the cold drink. "Mmm, they are both *gut*."

"I'm just going to put Leah down for a nap, but I'll be right back."

She laid Leah in her downstairs crib and returned to the kitchen.

She poured herself a glass of lemonade and joined the bishop at the table. "It's a hot day for visiting."

"Indeed. Tell me, May, does Thad work the farm every day, and do you cook his meals?"

A chill ran up her back. *"Jah."*

"How's this situation working out for you?" He took another sip and waited for her reply.

"I'm not sure I understand the question, Bishop." She rubbed her finger down the glass through the condensation.

"Jah, he jilted you years ago, is that right? So is it uncomfortable for you to live here? Together?"

"This is my family farm that Thad inherited from April, but *Daed* said I could stay here until I married."

"But he's here all day." The bishop gestured with his hand to the outside.

"He lets me stay, so I watch Leah and cook the meals. That's all. Otherwise, I see very little of him during the day."

The bishop finished his refreshment, pushed his chair back and gave May a nod. "See you on Sunday."

She froze in her chair, and waited until his footfalls left the porch. She looked out the window. What was that all about? Why was he asking such questions?

May sipped her lemonade, sat the glass down and dried her hand on her apron. No doubt, she wouldn't like the answers to those questions.

Thad took off his straw hat, slapped it against his leg to shake the dust and soil off, and plunked it back on his head. He watched the *youngies* he'd hired to pick vegetables leave for the day, then he sealed the cartons of tomatoes, beans and peas going to market.

It was a hot day, but at least it hadn't rained. He'd prayed for a sunny day, and *Gott* had answered. He sighed as his mind drifted to May.

They had started getting along, putting

the past behind them. At least he hoped so. Their conversations seemed more relaxed, and she was at least still considering staying. Maybe her hesitation to make a decision about moving was due to the thought of leaving Leah.

The shed door squeaked open and pulled his attention to footfalls approaching. He tried to hold back a smile. *Jah*, May was coming out to talk. He peered over his shoulder, then jerked around in surprise as he saw the bishop approaching. "Bishop Yoder, *hullo*."

"*Hullo*, Thad. I was visiting with May. She made some delicious banana bread and lemonade. Did you have some?"

"Ah, no, not yet, probably for supper. What brings you out here today?"

"An elder brought it to my attention that you and May were still living together."

Thad's back stiffened. "*Nein*, we aren't living together. I inherited her family's farm, and my parents are staying in the *dawdi haus.* Why bring this up now? April has been dead a year."

"Exactly, your year of mourning is over and now it is not acceptable. So you live in the *dawdi haus* with them?"

"I still sleep in the same bedroom that April and I shared."

The bishop kicked at a few peas that had landed on the floor before aiming his gaze at Thad. "To others in our district, they think this is not a *gut* arrangement. You are here all day and all night unchaperoned in the same *haus.* I heard that she was moving to Shipshewana to live with an *aent*?"

"*Jah,* that's what she said, but I think she is having a hard time leaving Leah."

"Is it just Leah that she is having the hard time leaving?"

Thad took a step back and clenched his teeth, then released. "I'm not sure I understand what you are talking about, Bishop."

"You courted May before you married her sister, *jah*?" The bishop's tone was the one he used for preaching.

"What are you saying, Bishop?" A rigidness seized Thad's shoulders.

"It's time May was married."

Thad felt the blood drain from his face.

The bishop walked to the door, then glanced back over his shoulder. "You need to think seriously about how this living arrangement looks to others. It cannot be allowed to go on much longer." The bishop walked out, letting the barn door bang closed.

Thad stared after him and scrubbed his hands over his face. *Why,* Gott, *why have You done this? I was hoping May would decide to stay but this...this will drive her away. And if the bishop finds out Elmer is always hanging around, he'll try to matchmake them. I had hoped to win her back.*

The next morning, Thad's gut clenched when he saw Elmer's buggy pulling into the drive. What did he want? But he already knew. *May.*

Perhaps the bishop had sent Elmer out

here to see May. Thad settled his feet like a bulldog with his paws planted squarely in the center of the walkway.

"*Gut morgen*, Thad." Elmer smiled as he approached.

Thad nodded. "Elmer. What brings you out this way?"

"Come to help May in her garden and visit with her a while."

Thad shot Elmer a cold stare, stepped off the walkway and stalked across the barnyard, the dust flying off the heels of his boots. He grabbed his toolbox off the shed's workbench and headed back to the *haus*.

He shook his head and tried to clear May out of his brain. She had a right to a life of her own but all he could see were her smoky-gray eyes staring at Elmer. Those same eyes made his heart swell until he could hardly breathe. Her hair and skin smelled like strawberry blossoms on a sunny June day.

He took the porch steps two at a time,

stopped and caught his breath before entering the kitchen. Bumping the screen door open with his hip, he maneuvered his toolbox through the doorway and set it on the floor, letting the door bang closed.

May and Elmer turned and scowled at his abrupt entrance. He looked up and locked on to her eyes, then let his gaze drop to her peaches-and-cream cheeks.

"What are you doing, Thad?" She squared her shoulders and lifted a brow. "Forget something?"

"*Nein.* I just remembered you wanted the doors fixed. Since Elmer was here, I thought it would be the perfect time to take off the swollen cupboard doors and fix them. Leah's door also sticks from the humidity. It squeaked when I opened it. We can take it off the hinges and plane a couple of spots to make it level. Since Elmer has two *gut* hands, I figured he'd want to help." Thad felt his face trying to smile but he controlled the urge.

Elmer pursed his lips and tossed Thad

a displeased stare. "*Jah*, okay. Let's get to it so I'll have a few minutes to visit with May."

"We'll start with the kitchen doors." Thad's instincts kicked in and told him he was in trouble, but he wasn't going to let Elmer have the upper hand before he tried to work things out with May.

He felt Elmer's glare as they finished up in the kitchen. Of course, he forgot a couple of tools and had to go to the shed twice. Thad nodded toward the stairway that led to the second floor and to Leah's room, but as he did, the glare in May's eyes and her furrowed brow signaled he'd upset her plans for a nice afternoon with Elmer.

Gut. A pang of uneasiness settled in his stomach. May deserved a nice man to court her, and Elmer was a *gut*-hearted man with many skills that kept him in demand, like his cheese business. But Elmer was also a stern man who worked his employees hard and no doubt would demand his *frau* do the same.

As Thad picked up his toolbox, he shot another glance in May's direction. A rosy blush tinged her cheeks like a January wind had just whirled through the room. She held her back straight as a yardstick and stared him down. He'd made his choice, married April, and now he should step aside and let May find happiness.

But he just couldn't. After speaking to the bishop, he wanted one more chance. With May.

Jah, he had no right disrupting her time with Elmer. Regret crept up his back but a smile curved his lips as he turned to head upstairs.

He had tossed May aside to marry April, now he was trying to prevent her from courting Elmer. What was wrong with him? Why did he keep hurting her? She was a *wunderbaar* woman any man would be proud to have as his *frau*.

Guilt pushed out a frustrated sigh, and his insides warred. He needed to back away and let May have her chance at happiness. Elmer needed his chance at winning May's heart. Thad owed her that, but why did it feel like a pitchfork was stabbing his heart?

May fumed under her breath as the men tromped up the stairs. She heard banging and pounding, feet shuffling around the wood flooring and a loud clink when the door hinge pin slid back into place.

When they came back downstairs, Elmer let out a loud sigh as he sat in the chair next to hers. Thad stomped toward the door, his toolbox clanging with tools shifting around as he gave her a nod. Her cheeks burned hot enough they could fry an egg.

"Job is done," Thad announced as he clomped out the door and down the porch steps.

May turned to Elmer. "I'm sorry you got roped into helping him."

"*Nein*, I wanted to help. Your cupboards are all fixed. I wouldn't want a loose door to swing open and bump your head when you weren't looking." He smiled like a *bu* who had just received a dollar to buy some candy.

"My cheese factory is doing very well." He glanced at May. "The artisanal cheese is a big seller. It's fancy cheese for the *Englisch*, they *liebe* it with crackers. The cheddar with bacon bits is my most popular seller. My shop is even in the Iowa Cheese Club and on the Iowa Cheese Roundup." He cleared his throat. "I'm building a *haus* and will be well established enough to marry soon."

The twinkle in his eye warned May he wasn't here just as her friend. She dropped her gaze as his hand started inching closer to hers. She jumped up, twisting her foot but stifled the yelp. "I'll make some coffee and we'll have a cookie. I made them the other day. Snickerdoodles."

"That's okay, May. Don't go to any trouble. Please, sit and talk."

"*Nein.* You deserve a little refreshment after driving all the way here and then helping Thad." She hurried to make a small pot of coffee, and in the meantime, set a plate of cookies on the table. When the coffee was ready, she poured two cups, set them on the table and collapsed on the chair.

"You seem tired, May."

"*Jah*, I am." When they finished their coffee, she stood and walked him to the porch. As she waved goodbye, a movement caught her eye and she turned toward the *dawdi haus.*

Gretchen was watching them from her flower garden.

It was for the best that he went home. She needed time to think of a way to tell Elmer she didn't *liebe* him and didn't want to marry him.

And she needed time to think of an answer for Thad…and what was best for the rest of her life.

Chapter Three

Thad helped his *youngies* stack the vegetable boxes of tomatoes, carrots and bush beans onto the truck bound for Des Moines. This load would complete the contract he had with a local market chain. He heaved the last box up into the waiting hands of the Vickerson Transport Company man inside the truck, stacking and securing the boxes. Done.

The truck driver handed Thad the clipboard with the receipt. He reviewed it, signed it, took his copy and handed it back. It was 6:30 a.m. when the truck pulled away.

Thad pulled a hanky from his pocket and wiped his brow as he watched the truck pull out of the drive. "Ethan Lapp, you and Carl Ropp head to the barn and start milking, it's getting late. The rest of you are on cleanup, follow me."

While Thad supervised, the *buwe* cleaned the packaging room of vegetable scraps, foam pieces and boxing debris, then he had them scrub the area and store the un-used cartons back on the shelves. When they completed the task, he had them dis-infect the milking room when Ethan and Carl had finished with the last cow. After lunch, they spent the rest of the day weed-ing the north forty acres. At four o'clock, he gathered the three summer hires for a short meeting. "*Danki* for all your help, you work hard and did a *gut* job today. You can come back on Friday morning for your pay. If you don't make it, I'll drop your check in the mail."

Daniel, the newest of his summer hires, stepped forward while the other two walked away. "*Danki*, Mr. Hochstetler. If you need help with anything else, give a shout."

Thad patted him on the back. "*Danki.* I'll do that."

As the *buwe* stood by their buggies talking, Thad overheard a few discussions of what they were going to do with their money. He chuckled. Most planned to save it. However, a few sounded like they were going to fix up their buggies to attract a pretty *mädel*.

Rumbling wheels on the drive pulled his attention from the *buwe* to his *daed*'s buggy heading straight toward him. *Daed* parked under the shade of the oak tree and stepped down. He walked toward Thad with an uneasy look on his face.

"Something wrong, *Daed*?"

The older man took a couple of purposeful strides closer. "The bishop stopped to chat with me in town." He kicked a stone with his foot as he stopped abruptly. "He said the elders didn't like you and May living in sin together. Your year of mourning is over. What was allowed before, won't be tolerated now."

Thad's jaw dropped. "That's not true."

Daed held up his hand. "Stop right there. Whether you are or not, it goes by appearance and what's decent. You're out here on the farm with May inside the *haus*. You wander in and out all day and spend the evenings together."

"Who said that?" Thad's back bolted up straight.

"Is it true or not?"

"*Jah*, but it's my *haus* and May lives here, too. It was her *daed*'s farm, but you know all that."

"You must marry May, or she must move out. I know what her papa said about her staying in the *haus*, but no doubt, he would thank me for looking out for her reputation. I worry that no nice *bu* will want to marry her."

Thad stepped back so fast he almost fell. His hands and face turned cold as his blood drained to his feet. His throat tightened so he could barely speak. "Who…is spreading rumors?"

"The bishop said that several elders have mentioned it to him. Not just that, but he doesn't want the *Englisch* neighbors to think that we condone living in sin. Not my words, his." *Daed*'s voice turned sullen. "Did you tell May that the bishop paid you a visit?"

"She knows he was here, but we never talked about what he said." Thad's gaze dropped to the grass. His mind whirled. He didn't want to lose May when they were just starting to get along. This would humiliate her, and for sure and for certain she'd move the three hundred miles to *Aent* Edna's.

Thad rubbed a hand over his heart. It felt as though a hundred stampeding Holsteins had trampled on his chest. Gott, *how do I make May understand? We need to get married—and fast. When I tell her, please ease her pain and confusion.*

He paced the ground, then faced his *daed*. "How much time did the bishop say we could have to think about this situation?"

Daed hooked his thumbs under his suspenders and locked eyes with Thad. "She has to be told today. Either she moves out in the next couple of days, or you marry." He gave Thad an easy pat on the shoulder. "She's a fine woman and would make Leah a *gut mamm*. Do what's right, Thad." He nodded and headed back to his buggy.

Thad wandered to the bench he'd made a year ago and sat in the front yard. He stared at his *daed*'s buggy kicking up dirt and sticks as it sped across the barnyard to the *dawdi haus*. The dust swirled in the wind, then disappeared like May would probably do when he told her about the gossip.

He kicked at the grass underfoot. He could give May back the farm, and she could pay someone to run it. The outcome would no doubt be the same. Someone would gossip about her and that man. Then the bishop would make her marry him.

They were getting along better. Maybe she'd consider a proposal. *Nein*, what was he thinking? She had told him once she hated her sister's secondhand clothes. She'd never want her secondhand husband.

He stood and walked around the *haus* toward the porch while a million reasons why their marriage was a bad idea bombarded his senses. Was it possible one of the *buwe* who worked for him was gossiping about him and May and his *daed* just didn't tell him?

He reached the porch steps and halted, one foot still in mid-air, then he slowly lowered it to the step. He tried to budge the other foot from the ground, but it felt as if glue clung to the sole of his shoe making the task difficult. Finally, one step after the other, he reached the top, knocked on the kitchen door and entered.

May glanced his way, then finished taking Mason jars from the processing kettle.

She checked the Kerr lids and set the jars to cool. She pushed the previous cooled jars to the back of the counter out of the way. She wiped her hands on a towel and turned from the sink. "Why did you knock, Thad? Did you want me to come out and help with something?"

"*Nein,* we need to talk."

"Let me dish up the food and we can talk during dinner. Leah's napping so it gives us a few minutes." May set the bowl of boiled potatoes next to the meatballs, sauerkraut, green beans and cinnamon bread already on the table. She pulled her chair from the table, letting the legs scrape against the wood flooring, then sat. They bowed their heads for silent prayer.

Thad rubbed his hands across his trousers. "It was a warm one today." His voice shook on the last word. *Lord, please help me say what I must.* After taking a bite, he took his napkin and blotted his mouth. "Mmm. This is delicious, but then your cooking is always *gut.*"

The hot food and warm kitchen teamed to coat his brow in perspiration. He swallowed hard, laid his fork down, took a deep breath, and told May about the bishop's visit the other day and the bishop's conversation with his *daed* today.

Her face went blank and her smoky-gray eyes turned stormy black.

"May, I adore you. I cared for you, *nein*, I loved you in a way when we courted, and I think you cared for me, too. We can get that back if we work at it. I'd like you to marry me. But if the answer is *nein*…then you'll have to move out of the *haus*."

His words speared May in the heart. "Who is gossiping about us?"

"If the bishop told *Daed*, he never told me." Thad lowered his gaze. "I must say, you're not as surprised as I thought you'd be." He raised his chin to face her again.

"Your *daed* never indicated who complained, or maybe named a neighbor?" Her eyes locked with his.

"*Nein.* It might be one of the *buwe* that work on the farm. Maybe they told the bishop, or their folks, that I walk in and out of the *haus* whenever I please without knocking or something like that. Did they ever stop to think, it is my *haus*, and you are only the...nanny?"

May's heart nearly stopped. *Only the nanny?*

"Look, May, I care about you, and I owe it to April to take care of you. We can get married and all will be well. What do you say?"

May stared at him in utter disbelief.

Leah let out a cry from her crib in the other room. She hurried and picked her up, changed her and snuggled her close as a tear threatened but May batted it away. How was she going to survive without seeing this sweet little girl?

She carried Leah to the kitchen, and set her down in the high chair. "I'll get her food ready so we can talk." She got her food and set her plate and cup on her tray.

"Okay, where were we?"

"May, you didn't answer my question."

She swallowed hard and looked Thad in the eye. "Before April died, she asked me to take care of her *boppli*. I stayed here to do just that, instead of going to Indiana, where *Mamm*'s family lives. Now I'm repaid by my friends and neighbors gossiping about me?"

"I—I'm sure it's not like that..." Thad stuttered.

"*Nein*, apparently it is." A knot tightened in the pit of her stomach. "I appreciate your offer of marriage, Thad, but that would keep you from marrying someone you loved."

"*Nein*. I did not say it right before. I *liebe* you and want to marry you. We could make it work, May. If I hadn't married April, we might have..." He stopped.

Her cheek twitched and heat rushed up her neck and burned all the way to her ears. She was sure her eyes shot lightning bolts.

In the silence, the ticking of the kitchen clock pulsed like the heartbeat of the *haus*.

Her life had just changed in a few seconds. The *haus*, the farm, Leah… Thad had everything. She had nothing once again. At least he'd given her a place to stay, for a little while anyway. Now, *Gott* had taken that away, too, but He stretched out two roads before her and she must choose.

"Thaddaeus Thomas Hochstetler. What's going on? You should be in the field."

May jerked around at the same time Thad did to see Gretchen with her hands perched on her hips.

"*Mamm*, people are gossiping about us living together, and we are discussing whether to marry or not."

"You want to marry May? *Nein*. She's nothing like her sister." Gretchen huffed and glanced at the dozen jars of canned string beans on the counter, then her gaze dropped to the bucket sitting on the floor still full of beans to be canned. "April worked twice as fast as her."

A flash of heat stormed through May's body as she listened to Gretchen berate her. Ha, three votes against staying: Edna's offer was one, her discomfort around Thad was two, and now Gretchen's unkind words.

Thad grabbed his *mamm*'s arm and escorted her out of the *haus*. When he stomped back into the kitchen, his face was as pale as a whitewashed fence.

"I have a lot to think about, Thad. Can you look after Leah for a little while?"

He nodded. "I'm sorry about all this, May."

Before she reached the stairs, Leah started to cry. She stopped and glanced at Thad. "You sure you're okay with her?"

"*Jah*, we're *gut*."

Before May reached the stairs, Leah was crying. This was a *gut* test for Thad to see how he handled his *tochter* on his own.

May closed her bedroom door and collapsed on the bed. She didn't want to marry Thad. She didn't love him. She could barely talk to him.

But she loved Leah and that little *mädel* loved her like a mama. She could sell her rag rugs to help Thad and she could bake bread, rolls, pies and cookies and sell them at her roadside stand.

But the whole idea was just crazy. She and Thad didn't *liebe* each other, not anymore, if they ever did.

She could hear Leah crying downstairs, then the sniffling grew closer, and closer and stopped. A tap sounded on her door.

She hesitated, then opened it. "Janie, what are you doing here?"

"That's a nice greeting for a friend. I hadn't seen you for a while so thought I'd stop by on my way to town. *Mamm* keeps me busy canning, but I wanted to see you. Thad said you were up here doing some thinking. He couldn't quiet this one's crying." Janie gave Leah a squeeze.

Leah sniffled and held her arms out

to May, sobs rocking her little shoulders while her nose ran. When Janie handed her over, Leah almost jumped into May's arms.

May enveloped her in a hug, then wiped the tears and her nose. Leah laid her head on May's shoulder with her arm stretched around her neck. "Shh. Everything will be okay."

May pointed toward the bed and her friend sat. She confided her dilemma and watched Janie gasp with each new piece of information.

"What are you going to do? If you ask me, I think you should give Thad a second chance," Janie whispered. "I think he's cute, and I've always liked him. Plus, he's tall with a muscular back and strong arms. Now, what *mädel* could resist that?"

"You're guy crazy." May lifted a brow. "I believe I have two choices—marry Thad or move to Shipshewana, where I would probably never see Leah again. And right now, she is the only joy in my life."

"The decision to marry is for life. Amish don't get divorced. I know you realize that, but I just wanted to remind you. Oh, here's another idea. If they have a lot of *gut*-looking guys in Indiana, send me a letter, and I'll move out there with you." Janie chuckled.

May rolled her eyes at her sweet and funny friend. "Again, you're guy crazy. The scary thing is, I've never been to Shipshewana, and I have no idea if I will like Indiana."

"You know you could always come back later, if you weren't happy there. I'll pray for you, May, but here is something else to consider. Your sister, Sadie, is pregnant with twins. I heard she was looking for a mother's helper, so you could go live with her. She'll soon have five *kinner* all under the age of five. Oh, but you'll have to share a room with Sadie's oldest, your niece Isabelle. What do you say? Think about it. I'm sure Sadie would *liebe* to see you come and stay."

May laughed. "I'm glad you stopped by. You certainly cheered me up." She gave Janie a one-armed hug.

"If you move, can I have Thad?" Janie's eyes widened almost as much as her smile.

May ignored the question. "If I go to *Aent* Edna's, I'll be working in a bakery for the rest of my life. That is, unless I find someone in Indiana to marry. Or I could stay here with this little bundle of joy that I *liebe* like a heartbeat." She gave Leah a jiggle up and down and listened to her musical giggle. "No more tears when you're with *aentie*, huh? I've prayed, but *Gott* has been silent so far."

"*Jah*, He might want you to search your heart, May, or He might want to see if you'll reason it out and make a practical decision. Here's another offer—come and live with us. *Mamm* would *liebe* another pair of hands to help out around the *haus*."

Footsteps echoed in the hall followed by a knock on the door. "May? I need to talk to you for a second." Thad's voice cracked.

Janie put a hand on May's shoulder. "I need to go, but if you want to talk later, stop by the *haus*. I'll see you on Church Sunday."

May opened the door and her friend slipped out, waving as she flew down the hallway. "Sorry, Thad, you're probably starved since our lunch got spoiled with talking. I can warm lunch back up."

"*Nein*, that's not why I'm here. The bishop is downstairs waiting to see you."

May's heart dropped to her stomach. "What?"

"*Jah*, I'll just take Leah and walk over to the *dawdi haus*. Give you some privacy."

May made her way downstairs and into the kitchen. The bishop sat at the kitchen table but nodded when she entered.

"*Hullo*, May. I'd like a minute of your time, if you're not too busy." The bishop casually sipped a mug of coffee that smelled as if Thad had warmed the leftover brew from lunch.

"Bishop, what can I do for you?" She sat,

rested her elbows on the table and clasped her hands.

He shot her a stern look. "I drove out to see which day next week I should clear in my schedule for your wedding."

Chapter Four

Thad's heart felt stretched, as if he wore it on the soles of his shoes and he was walking on it. If May decided to move to Indiana, what would he do without her? He and Leah would both miss her.

May loved Leah and he hoped enough to stay and marry him. If they married, he'd shower her with so much happiness, she'd have no choice but to fall in *liebe* with him again.

But if May ever found out the real reason why he married April, she would hate him.

A lump rose in his throat. What if May

decided to move away, and he never saw her again? She was the only woman he wanted.

He glanced at the clock. One hour past the last time he looked. What was the bishop saying that it was taking so long?

Ethan entered the barn, letting the door bang as he walked toward Thad. "I'll start the evening milking, Mr. Hochstetler."

Thad nodded. "*Gut*. I'll help, and you can follow me." *Jah*, he needed to concentrate on something to keep his mind off May. He applied the iodine mixture to the cows' udders while Ethan followed along behind with the alcohol wipe. Ethan was a *gut bu* and a hard worker. Thad appreciated the loyalty the young man gave him.

He finished his barn chores, stepped out of the barn and noticed the bishop's buggy still parked in his drive. He heaved a long sigh. It was not a *gut* sign that the bishop was still talking to May. That could only mean one thing—May said no and the bishop was trying to talk her into marrying him.

When the screen door banged closed, Thad gave a grunt and walked toward the bishop's buggy. His heart pounded like a blacksmith's hammer with every step.

The bishop met him at his buggy wearing a long face. Then he smiled at Thad. "*Jah*, she will marry you in two weeks. Since you have been married before, and her *mamm* and *daed* have passed away, she wants just a small gathering instead of inviting the whole community. Until then, you will sleep in the *dawdi haus*. I'll read the banns on Sunday."

After the bishop left, he felt numb. This seemed too *gut* to be true. He inched his way to the *haus*, pulled the screen door open, entered the kitchen and stopped cold. May was standing at the sink, her back toward him. He gawked at her, unsure what to say. Should he wait for her to speak first? His gut clenched as he pulled a chair away from the table and sat.

Though it was summer outside, a coolness filled the distance between them. Was she going to back out?

Had she truly forgiven him?

The minute she turned from the sink, his heart raced, and his tongue felt like a piece of toast. He stood up, his knees shaking, when she approached the table.

"*Hullo.*"

He nodded and smiled.

May motioned for him to sit. She sat across from him, laid her hands in her lap and straightened her back. "Were you surprised to hear the news from the bishop?"

"*Jah*, but *gut* surprised." He dropped his gaze to his hands folded on the table and studied them. Each callus, each skinned knuckle and each chipped nail had a story. He raised his eyes to hers. "I have just one question. Your answer won't stop the wedding, but I want to know…are you marrying me because you have forgiven me, or because you *liebe* Leah too much to leave her?" He held his breath for a second before blowing it out.

May glanced at the window, then returned her gaze to him. Her demeanor seemed more businesslike than happy that she'd just accepted a marriage proposal.

His pulse quickened. Something wasn't right. Had the bishop threatened a shunning or something if she didn't marry him?

He bit his lip and braced for the worst.

Silence stretched across the room. All he could hear was the pounding of his heart. It just occurred to him…he might not like what she was going to say.

Dampness beaded his brow.

May's heart nearly stuttered to a stop. "Thad…" She kept her gaze on her hands, then lifted her eyes to meet his. "I'm not going to lie to you or pretend this is something that it's not. I'll tell you the truth, and if you want to call off the wedding afterward, that's fine. I'll understand and move to Indiana."

He shifted in his chair, and she noticed the moisture dotting his forehead. Maybe she should have made this easy and bought a train ticket to Shipshewana.

"Listen, Thad. April asked me to take care of you and Leah, but she didn't tell me to marry you. Two things are keeping me in Iowa. I want to be the one to raise Leah, and I want to help you save the farm."

She peered into his face, then glanced away. He looked shocked. "Not quite what you wanted to hear?"

"I'm listening."

"Scripture tells us we must forgive or *Gott* will not forgive us. It's hard, but if He said I must, then I will… I have. Yet at times, like when I look at Leah and see your features, it floods back into my memory that you tossed me aside for April." Her voice quaked.

"May." Thad started to speak, but she held up a hand.

"You said you loved me. I'm not sure about that, but maybe so. We were always the best of friends. Back then, did we even know what *liebe* was? But if you had truly loved me, you wouldn't have married my sister. You'd have married me."

Discomfort lined his face.

"I'll try to make you a *gut frau*. It might take some time, but maybe after a while, I'll be able to put the past behind us and move on. But I can't promise that on some days it won't surface. If this doesn't work for you, I'll leave tomorrow."

"*Nein*, I want you for my *frau*, and I will do everything in my power to make you forget the past." He unclasped his hands on the table and reached his right hand across to her. She slowly put her hand in his. He clasped his fingers around hers and squeezed, then she squeezed. "The bargain is sealed."

Her cheeks burned and her heart nearly stuttered to a stop.

"We'll be married in two weeks and have the service here on the farm." His eyes held hers captive for several seconds before letting go.

He pulled his hand slowly away from

hers as he stood, and a lonely feeling gripped her as he walked away.

She brought her hand to her face, curled her fingers and braced the knuckles against her chin as her elbow rested on the table. May took a deep breath and could smell the lingering scent of soiled straw.

The next day, May called her sister, *aents* and close friends to tell them her big news. Sadie insisted everyone come to her farm for the planning.

The following day dawned with a brilliant sun to chase away her cloudy mood. Fear started to shimmy up her spine. Had she made the right decision? She could still buy a train ticket. *Nein*, she shook his hand. She'd made a bargain.

She forced those thoughts from her head and hitched Gumdrop, her favorite horse, to her buggy and headed to her sister Sadie's farm to plan the wedding. The clip-clop of Gumdrop's hooves had a calming effect. She watched the yards of daffodils and roses go by, the birds sitting on the fence chirping take flight, and the occasional motor vehicle zip past.

She guided Gumdrop up the drive and passed the toolshed. John, Sadie's *ehemann*, greeted her with a wave. "Mornin'."

"*Hullo*, May. Congratulations. Sadie is excited and started planning without you so you better hurry on in."

"*Danki*, John. That's what big sisters are for." She laughed as she ran to the *haus*.

Sadie flung open the door. "*Ach*, May, I can't believe you and Thad are getting married. I had no idea you two were back together. That's so *wunderbaar*."

Her *aents* and cousins from her *daed*'s side were there and took over the planning while May worked on her wedding dress. It would have been nice if *Aent* Edna could have made it, and her other relatives from Indiana, but it was too short notice to make travel plans. And some of her cousins didn't have the extra money for such things.

She held up her dress. It was the same

material as her Sunday dress, only this one was in her favorite shade of blue. A sense of hope seemed to cling to the cloth as she laid it down and ran her hand down the bodice. A string of emotions wheezed through her one right after the other. Regret, turned to excitement, then slid into nervousness. Moisture gathered and clogged her throat. *Mamm, I wish you could have been here to see me married.* At the sound of shuffling feet, she cleared her throat and fluttered her eyelids to bat away the extra moisture.

"May, congratulations." *Aent* Matilda whirled into the room with her *tochter* Josephine close behind. "We are so happy for you."

"*Danki* for coming, and Josie, *danki* for being one of my attendants."

"Cousin, I'm thrilled you asked me. I'm so excited for you." Josie knelt on the floor beside May's chair and squeezed her hand. "This is so *wunderbaar*, and now Leah will have a real *mamm*."

Matilda flounced into a chair next to May. "*Jah*, and Josie and I will organize your kitchen help and see that all the food is prepared on time. Your wedding will be a very special day, indeed."

Matilda gave May a one-armed hug and shared what May's *mamm* and *daed*'s wedding day was like. The day flowed with joy and excitement, and Matilda remembered the stars in both her parents' eyes. "*Jah*, now we must go and help plan and prepare and you must finish your dress." She patted May's hand as she stood.

The air stilled after Matilda and Josie swished through the room like a broom, and May stared at her wedding dress and the stitch she just made. Her hands shook as she stuck the needle in the hem of the dress. It was really happening. She was going to marry Thad. Her heart beat fast and hard, but she wasn't quite sure why. It was only a marriage of convenience. *Nein.* A marriage bargain. Nothing more.

Before she'd left the farm, Thad had

given the *youngies* instructions to clean the yard and barnyard, and when they finished with that, they were to start plucking the chickens for the wedding dinner. The women were planning to serve baked chicken, mashed potatoes, gravy, creamy celery casserole, coleslaw, pies, donuts, pudding and several cakes, which included two special ones that her friend Sarah and her sixteen-year-old *tochter* Mary would make.

When she got home from Sadie's, it was non-stop work of washing walls, floors, fixtures, dusting from top to bottom, borrowing dishes and silverware, and planning the seating to feed one hundred guests. Although Matilda had organized and delegated a job to each of her cousins, May still insisted on helping. Most Amish weddings would have as many as three to four hundred guests. When an average Amish family was nine people, it didn't take long to fill the guest book. *Aent* Matilda and Josie were in charge of organizing the kitchen and cooks and May knew not to interfere.

Since Thad's farm had belonged to her parents, it made sense for her wedding to take place there.

On the eve of her wedding, May twirled around in her room like it was the last time she'd ever see it. Of course it wasn't, but why was that feeling stirring in her stomach? She stopped moving and blotted a tear that had collected in the corner of her eye. She glanced out the window and toward heaven. How she wished *Mamm* and *Daed* could be here with her right now. But if they were, what would they truly think about her marrying Thad? Would *Daed* have given his blessing?

May woke early and bolted upright in bed. Ach, *it's my wedding day!* A shiver of fear swept over her. Had she made the right decision? It wasn't too late; she could change her mind.

Nein, she'd given her word.

She jumped out of bed and slipped into her wedding dress. The noise from downstairs with Matilda and her helpers preparing food for the noon wedding meal seeped through the floor.

May took special care with her hair, pinning it back and into a bun as her *mamm* had taught her when she was young. She carefully placed her new prayer *kapp* in just the exact place. This would be the only time she'd wear these clothes, then she'd pack them away for her funeral.

May smoothed her skirt and slipped her apron over it. The *Englisch* liked to wear fancy dresses to their weddings, but she was content with the Plain ways. If everyone in her community wore Plain clothes, then no one would appear wealthier than another, and she liked that thought.

A tap sounded on her bedroom door. "May? Open up, it's Janie and Josie."

She ran to the door and threw it open. "I'm so glad you're both here." She wrapped them each in a group hug, then stepped back. "How do I look?"

"That blue is the perfect color for you," Josie said, and Janie nodded in agreement.

"Are you getting cold feet?" Janie raised a brow. "Your face is saying take me out behind the barn and hide me."

"*Ach*, just a little bit. I hope this is the right choice. The bishop pressured me to make a decision, and now I'm not sure."

"Don't worry, you'll be fine. You've liked Thad ever since you were fourteen."

"*Jah*, but don't forget, he married April first."

Josie grabbed May's hand and held it tight. "Forgive like Jesus did."

"I'm trying." She glanced at the clock on her nightstand, then turned to her side-sitters. "It's almost nine o'clock… We'd better go downstairs."

They hurried to their bench in the family room as Thad and his attendants, his brothers Jonah and Simon, took their places.

At 9:00 a.m., the congregation started to

sing the first song from the *Ausbund* while the ministers motioned to Thad and May to follow them to the back room, or rightfully called the council room for her wedding, for their twenty-minute premarital talk. Her stomach clenched as she stood. She'd seen other couples get marched off, but no one ever divulged what a twenty-minute talk was, not even Sadie. But it was considered part of the ceremony so it had a great significance. She blotted her hand on her skirt as the ministers entered the room first. Thad pressed a warm hand to her back as they entered. His strong support and nearness calmed her, knowing she wasn't in this alone. He turned and closed the door.

When they stepped from the room, Thad grabbed her hand and walked beside her. May almost jerked her hand away, but didn't. They were a couple now. They returned to their benches. Thad and his two attendants sat and faced May and her side-sitters.

After the ministers gave their sermons, Bishop Yoder delivered the main sermon that focused on the Old Testament marriages, their relationships and the obstacles their marriages faced. Just before noon, the bishop called May and Thad up front for the wedding ceremony.

Thad said his vows first.

The bishop glanced toward May. "Do you promise…?"

May froze. The words wouldn't come. Her heart raced and her throat tightened. She drew in a deep breath of air, but her throat was too tight to speak.

Thad stared at May with a pale mask covering his face. "May?"

"*Jah*, take your time, May," Bishop Yoder whispered.

May squeezed her eyes closed. What was it Janie said? This was final. Forever. What was she thinking? She should have thought about this longer.

A faint shuffling of feet from someone

on the benches caught her attention. *Jah,* she had to answer.

The bishop touched her elbow. "Do you need to sit?"

"*Nein.* I feel better."

The bishop repeated the question.

She cleared her throat. "Yes."

Bishop Yoder quickly pronounced them *ehemann* and *frau.* May froze as his words settled over her like a thin dusting of flour. It was real. She was Thad's *frau.*

After the closing words, Thad took her hand and pulled her gently to face him. "Don't look so scared. We are now one, forever and always, May." He pulled the back of her hand to his lips and bushed it with a kiss. A smile slowly spread across his face until it reached his eyes and tugged at May's heart.

She turned her head trying to hide her face, until she finally gave in and smiled back.

When Mildred's helpers had everything

ready, she called to the wedding party to take their places at the bridal table.

They sat at the *Eck*, the bridal table, and ate their meal. There was little talking since everyone was hungry after the long morning. May took a sip of lemonade and let her gaze wander to Thad. He was talking to his *bruder* Jonah. She hadn't really paid much attention lately, but when he was cleaned up, he was a handsome man, her *ehemann*.

May turned toward Josie and Janie and joined in on their discussion, chattering as if they were at a frolic.

Thad reached over and gave May's arm a quick pat.

She pulled her attention from her side-sitters and focused on Thad. Her face twisted into a playful smile.

"It will be nice having a *frau*. Now I won't have to take out the garbage." His voice teetering toward the loud side.

Knowing he was trying to break the tension between them, she tossed him a not-on-your-life look with a raised brow. "You're not getting off that easy." They both chuckled.

Their laughter lightened the mood, and it helped May forget that he was April's *ehemann* first and she was once again getting April's hand-me-down clothing. Only this time it was her husband.

Thad glanced at her. "Are you sure you're okay, May?"

"*Jah*, it's just…my head is spinning. Two weeks ago, I had planned to buy a train ticket to Indiana. Now I'm married."

"But you're okay with it, right?" He caught her hand in his and squeezed.

"I'm fine."

"We need to walk around and greet our guests." He swung his legs over the bench and pulled her to her feet, wrapping his arm around her.

She shook aside the image of April eighteen months earlier, in this very spot, and clung to Thad's side as they walked around all afternoon and evening visiting with their guests.

When the last few buggies finally pulled away, Thad helped the *youngies* pick up the benches, and May stole her way back into the *haus* and up to Leah's room. She cracked the door and peeked in.

Josie, dressed in her nightgown, sat next to Leah's crib. She waved her in.

"I missed this little one," Josie whispered.

"Me, too." May quietly pulled the rocker over next to Josie's chair by the crib and sat.

"You should be with your new *ehemann*." Josie nodded toward the door. "I'm watching Leah. Go."

"I just wanted to check on her. He is helping the *buwe* stack the benches on the wagon so they'll be ready for Church Sunday."

"How does it feel to be a *frau*?"

The question bounced around in her head. She wasn't quite sure of the answer.

She wanted to be Leah's *mamm*, and Thad came along as baggage. "It's a new feeling."

That was a lie. She felt numb.

Josie gave her a hug. "I'll help clean the mess tomorrow. You go get ready for bed. You're a married woman now. I'll sleep on the twin bed next to Leah's crib. And don't worry about a thing."

May slid out of the rocker, walked to the door, and glanced back at Josie and Leah. Leah looked like a little angel, and after the long day, Josie looked like she was asleep already.

She hoped her married life was as simple as that.

Chapter Five

At noon a week later, Thad looked toward the *haus* and noticed May standing in the kitchen doorway waving her hand vigorously to get his attention. He stopped the buggy and stepped down to hear her words.

"Dinner is ready," she said with a pleasant voice but a weak smile tugged at the corners of her mouth.

The past week had been tense. May had married him, but ever since that day, she'd acted as if it were a mistake. He certainly didn't profess to know the mind of a woman, but if he had to guess, it seemed like she regretted her bargain.

Thad crossed the lawn and headed up the porch steps, dread dragging his heels. Another dreary lunch with May, watching her stare at her food until it was gone, then she'd jump out of her chair and start clearing the table. Anything else was better than a conversation with him.

Where was all the happiness he was going to shower on his *frau*? Forcing this marriage had been a bad idea. But he knew if May ever left the farm, she'd never come back. He had to be patient and give her time to warm up to him. They had only been married a week.

He'd always heard that the first year of marriage was the hardest. Maybe everyone who said that was right.

He hung his hat on the rack, washed his hands and quickly scooted to his chair, trying to stay out of May's way in the kitchen. The scent of fried chicken, mashed potatoes and gravy wafted through the air, not her usual lunch menu. May was a terrific cook, and even if her company was lacking, her meal more than made up for her coolness.

After silent prayer, May cleared her throat. "Thad, I want to apologize for the way I've acted toward you this past week and your marriage to April." He could see the tears run down her cheeks. "There is no excuse for my actions. You are my *ehemann* now..." the word stumbled out "...Leah is now my daughter, and I'd like to try to get along. Start fresh again. The marriage happened so fast. I made a decision." Her voice cracked.

His face burned as shame inched its way up his back. He set his fork down and swallowed hard. "I'm sorry, too. I should have told you that April and I were getting married instead of letting you hear about it when they read the banns at church. That was wrong. Instead, all the unspoken words have been hanging between us, creating a big ugly storm cloud. I'm sorry it had to come to this."

She wiped a quick hand down her cheek and glanced his way. "*Jah*, I agree."

For the rest of the meal, May talked to him and even smiled. She chatted about the garden, the strawberries she had picked and her expectations that she'd have an ample amount for canning. "If you bring in some cream, I'll make strawberry ice cream. Leah would like that."

"*Jah*, okay."

After milking, Thad headed across the barnyard toward the north forty to see how the pickers were progressing in the field. The tomatoes were a bumper crop this year. That would help offset what he lost on the milk, but even a bumper crop wouldn't save it if he lost much more income.

He watched May carry a basket of laundry out to the clothesline. She shook out her dresses and hung them in a row next to his shirts.

His heart raced. The sudden urge struck him to run over to May, pull her into his arms and press a kiss to her lips. When she was nearby, he couldn't take his eyes off her. Her slim form and that auburn hair peeking out from beneath her prayer *kapp* made him want to stand here all day and watch her.

He swallowed hard. Sweat beaded on his forehead. He searched his shirt pocket for his hanky. Empty. He checked his pants pocket. Nope. He removed his hat and rubbed his shirtsleeve across his forehead.

Somehow, he had to get May to fall in *liebe*, but he could see that wouldn't be easy. *Jah*, she said she was sorry for the way she acted toward his marriage to April, but had she really forgiven him? Actions spoke louder than words. And some days she barely tolerated him. He'd bide his time and think of a way, but his arms were sure itching to hold her.

He swiped his stained and sweaty hat against his trousers, then thumped it back on his head. He glanced at May one more time before continuing to the field.

May finished hanging the laundry, grabbed the basket and headed for the *haus*. When she noticed Thad watching her, her heart gave a weird jump.

Lord, please grant me a double portion of patience and tolerance for Thad. Please help me stash my personal feelings and help save the farm. And sometimes, Lord, I feel I married Thad for the wrong reason. Forgive me.

As the week went on, she saw less and less of Thad as he stayed busy with the harvest. He ran in the *haus* for dinner and supper, then worked until dark, barely seeing May or Leah. *Jah*, she knew farmers were busy, but he had an obligation to his *tochter*, didn't he?

When Leah awoke from her nap, May peeked around the corner of the crib. "Peekaboo!"

Leah laughed and held out her arms.

"There's my big *mädel*. Would you like your diaper changed so you'll be all sweet-smelling for your *daed*? Some day, we will start potty training. Won't that be fun?"

"Nein." Leah giggled.

"Jah, it will be fun."

"Nein." She laughed at the game they were playing.

Leah's eyes brightened and she jabbered away. She didn't really know what the words meant, but it sounded like a great idea.

May reached out her arms. "Let's go see *Daed*."

She carried Leah to the barn. Walking through the barn, she heard noise coming from Tidbit's stall. She stuck her head around the corner and Leah followed suit.

Thad looked up and smiled. "Ah, so my two girls have come out to see me." He set his pitchfork against the wall, walked over and gave Leah a kiss on her head.

"Ew." May wrinkled her nose.

"Ew." Leah winkled her nose, than patted it with her hand.

"What brings you two out here? Wanting to help, maybe?"

She smiled. "Not hardly. Leah misses you. When you walk out the door, she watches it a long time for you to return. At least spend a little time with her when you come in to eat."

He nodded. "*Jah*, you're right. I'll spend some time with her at meals."

She held Leah out toward Thad. "Would you like to hold her now?"

"My hands are dirty and I'm smelly. Wait until I come in and clean up."

"Okay. Barbecued spare ribs will be ready in an hour." She wrinkled her nose and made the trip out of the barn faster than on the way in.

Thad smiled and shook his head as he watched May leave. For sure and certain, she didn't want him around but was willing to sacrifice her happiness for Leah. His heart ached each time he saw her sad eyes. How he longed to take her in his arms and hold her until her pain went away.

Whirling around to retrieve his pitch-fork, his foot smashed a bug that darted across his path. *Jah*, it was evident that May's love for him was as dead as that bug. But what did he expect? This was a marriage of convenience and nothing more. Unless he could strike a spark in her, but how would he go about doing that? Maybe there was another way to win her heart...

He finished cleaning Tidbit's stall and would tackle the others after dinner. Parking his boots by the barn door, he slipped his feet into his shoes and headed to the *haus*. May's barbecued ribs were his favorite.

After dinner, Thad picked up Leah and set her on his lap. Her little eyes stared up at him intently, studying his features. She'd brought along her baby doll and he had to hold that on his other leg. Leah reached for his whiskers, but Thad turned his head fast and they slipped through her fingers. She giggled and giggled. He turned back, she grabbed for them again and he jerked them away.

She laughed and squealed. *"Daed."*

"What did you say?"

She laughed and showed her little teeth.

"May, did you hear what she said?"

"Jah, it was plain as day, she said *Daed."*

Leah's tiny fingers gripped his blue chambray shirt as if she were the one keeping him safe and secure. His heart melted. He stroked his finger over her velvety soft cheek. There was nothing he wouldn't do for these two girls. But this wee one needed all the protection he could give her.

She giggled and squirmed around on his lap, playing with her doll. She finally set her doll down and leaned back against him, her eyelids slowly starting to droop. She popped them open, but slowly they closed in sleep.

The sound of a dish breaking in the sink

jerked his attention in time to see May lose her balance standing on a stool and fall. Her arms flying in every direction, she smacked hard against the sink, then crumpled to the floor. He hurried and laid Leah in her crib and ran back to help May.

She stuck her hand up. "*Nein*, don't touch me." She grunted as she tried to move. Then froze. And moaned as she slumped against the sink, her bottom firmly planted on the floor.

"Did you hurt your back?"

"*Nein*. I hit the sink with my arm and shoulder and probably bruised them *gut*. I twisted my ankle when I fell, so I can't stand on my left foot."

"Let me help you up, and I'll take a look."

"You're not touching me, Thad," she ground out through clenched teeth.

"Well, it's either that or I'm going to the barn to call an *Englisch* ambulance to take you to the hospital."

"Are you crazy? I'm perfectly fine." She

tried to stand but the movement and exertion caused a flush to rise on her cheeks. She inhaled three deep breaths. "I might need a little help."

"I'll put my arm around your waist and lift you straight up. If you want me to stop, just say so."

She threw him a glance with fear-filled eyes as the colored drained from her face.

"I'll try not to hurt you." *Jah*, like that was really going to happen. He could already see a huge lump on her foot, and the way she held her shoulder, it might be broken, too. "I'll try to inch you up slowly. Take a deep breath."

She inhaled deeply, and before she could exhale, he had her on her right foot holding the left up off the floor.

"What happened to the inching idea?" She groaned and her cheeks paled.

He touched her hand, then her cheeks. They were cold and clammy. Fear crept into his heart.

"I'm so weak. Let me sit and rest a minute."

He helped her to a chair and slowly lowered her down. "Okay. I'm calling a driver and taking you to the hospital. I think your foot is broken and maybe your shoulder, too." He held his voice steady, but inside, he was shaking like a fall leaf in the wind.

"I'm feeling a little better, but my foot really hurts." Her voice cracked. She tried to move it but he could see tears in her eyes.

"If it's broken, it will hurt until the doctor sets it. I'm going to the barn to use the emergency phone to call for a car. Leah is sleeping—will you be all right?"

"Yes."

Now he knew something was broken or she'd never have so readily agreed. He watched her for just a second to make sure she looked settled enough that he could leave her for a few minutes.

When he returned to the *haus*, he crouched down next to May. "Are you okay?"

Her voice shook. "Sure. What will we do with Leah, take her with us?"

"*Nein.* I called the neighbors, Caleb and

Sarah Brenneman. They'll come and pick her up. Since Sarah is pregnant, the bishop let them have a phone and Caleb just happened to be in the barn when I called."

"She'll be scared to go with someone she doesn't recognize." May heaved a nervous breath.

"I know, but it's probably time she got used to it. Something like this could happen again." The minute the words left his mouth, he wanted to bite them back.

"I certainly hope not." She cringed when she leaned back against the chair.

He propped a hip against the counter. "So do I, but we need to plan for what could happen."

"I know. I just think about how she will miss us." Her voice wavered with worry and pain.

"I need to go to the toolshed and write out instructions for the *youngies* I hired to help weed the crops this week. With the past few days of rain, the weeds are out of control." He left a note on the workbench, then hurried back to the barn to give Tidbit a quart of oats and fresh water. The strong smell of soiled straw assailed his nostrils. He'd neglected his maintenance duties while trying to get the fields worked, but mucking out the stalls would need to wait a couple more days.

When he entered the kitchen, May had her arm propped on the table, and the other lay next to it, the hand curled closed and white-knuckled. The gravel in the driveway crunched under buggy wheels and hooves. Thad glanced out the window. "Sarah and Caleb are here."

He opened the door as Sarah flew to May's side. No doubt, Sarah's years of experience in the bakery business had prepared her for many unforeseen emergencies. "May! How do you feel?"

"A little better. *Danki* for taking Leah."

"*Jah*, of course. I'll pack enough bottles and clothes for a few nights, and Caleb will take her mattress so she'll have a familiar place to sleep." Sarah and Caleb dashed upstairs and returned to the kitchen with the mattress and a box and bag stuffed with Leah's things. Caleb carried it all out to the buggy.

Sarah bustled over to the downstairs crib, picked up Leah, her eyes big and round with puzzlement, and snuggled the tyke close.

Leah puckered up to cry. "Shh, little one," Sarah cooed softly until Leah settled back in the crook of her arm and closed her eyes. "She'll be fine." Sarah was still crooning to her when she disappeared out the door and Caleb latched it closed.

Silence filled the room as May stared at the door.

Thad noticed May shift on her chair and a pained expression crossed her face, but not like the one when she fell. This look, he imagined, was more about separation anxiety from Leah. He turned toward the window as a lump lodged in his throat and watched the buggy pull out of the drive, nearly colliding with the SUV that pulled in.

"Our ride is here." He helped May get to her feet and wobble out to the SUV. He hadn't wrapped his arms around May since they'd married. It felt strange as the swish of her skirt touched his leg when he tugged her close to give her support. Her warmth and the smell of strawberry shampoo evoked a memory tucked safely away. Until now.

Gott, *don't let me stumble.* He had a plan to win May's forgiveness, not just in words but also in her heart, and he didn't want to ruin his chance.

Chapter Six

May held her breath. She squeezed Thad's hand tightly as she slipped into the SUV and settled on the seat. She blew out a long sigh. "My arm is so sore I can barely move it, and I can't step on my foot without excruciating pain. It's so swollen. What am I going to do if I'm in a cast? How will I take care of Leah or myself?"

"Take it easy and don't worry about all that. We'll be there in a few minutes." He tried to give her an encouraging look, but she could see he was worried, too.

The eighteen miles to Iowa City felt like it took hours. Each turn and sway of the vehicle caused pain to rip upward and over the top of her arm. She gasped and tried to watch the scenery passing by the window to take her mind off the trip. That didn't work. Her mind kept replaying Leah leaving the *haus* with Sarah and Caleb. Loneliness crept into May's heart knowing that little tyke wouldn't be there to greet her when she got home.

Her left hand moved to her temple and massaged the throbbing pain that had started there when Leah left the *haus*. Sarah would take *gut* care of Leah. Of that May had no doubt. But she still was worried about her.

The SUV jerked to a stop at the emergency entrance of the hospital and May bumped into Thad. She groaned.

"Are you okay?" He wrinkled his brow, then tossed the driver a warning look.

The man looked back over his shoulder. "Sorry about that."

Thad paid him, then helped May. She moaned and scooted to the edge of the seat, swung her legs around and pushed herself gently out of the SUV with her good arm, and gently eased into the waiting wheelchair that an attendant had pushed over to the vehicle.

With the advent of warmer weather, summer brought farm accident victims and several children with broken bones to the Emergency Room, all of whom were in line ahead of May to see the doctor.

"They'll call your name when it's time for your X-ray," the woman in Admitting said as she directed May to the waiting area.

Thad pushed May's wheelchair to a private corner away from the others. "Would you like some coffee?"

She nodded, and watched him saunter over to the coffee maker and pour her a cup. Guilt worked its way through her. What would she have done without Thad's help? She was hard on him, but this was the Thad she remembered, always so kind and willing to help a friend in need.

Jah, his tenderness was probably nothing more than a friend helping a friend. Except she wasn't only his friend. She was his *frau*. Like the bishop said, he was her forever helpmate.

May sat on a gurney in a cordoned-off area of the emergency room, waiting for the results of her X-ray. The cold room made her shiver all the way from her head to her feet. She grabbed the edges of the gurney with her left hand to support her aching body. The pain and soreness were making her tired. She wanted to lie down and sleep. If she could just rest a bit, she'd probably be fine.

She moved to the right, trying to get more comfortable. "Oh, it hurts to even move."

Thad walked over and stood next to her. "Lean on me."

She bumped against him and felt his warmth. His closeness stuttered her heart for a second. He slid his arm around her shoulder. "Feel better?"

She drew a ragged breath, but this time it wasn't from the pain. *"Jah, danki."*

The door opened and a handsome young man in a white coat hurried in and stuck out his hand. "I'm Dr. Kincaid. Nice to meet you, May. We're going to have you fixed up and on your way very soon. I'm just going to examine the injured areas."

He felt her shoulder, moved her arm around and looked at her hand. Then he took off her shoe, tenderly touched her ankle and examined her foot. He glanced up and looked at her face as he felt around. "What's your pain level from one to ten when I move your foot?"

"Maybe eight. If I try to stand on it a ten."

The doctor nodded. "Your shoulder and arm have bruising, but they're not broken. There is a lot of tissue damage so there will be discoloring and swelling for a few days."

He pushed a plastic-looking sheet onto a lighted box on the wall, then pointed.

"This is the X-ray of your foot. Right here, in the fourth metatarsal in the left foot, is a crack and a tiny chip out of the bone. We'll need to immobilize the ankle so it won't move and put pressure on the cracked bone. That will allow it to heal and prevent further injury."

"But, Dr. Kincaid, I have a one-year-old daughter. I can't be laid up a few weeks."

"I'm sorry, but you really don't have a choice. You could injure it further if you don't let it heal properly. I'm going to put your foot in a boot support and after the swelling goes down, you'll be able to move around comfortably. You'll have limitations, but you should still be able to care for a small child. Your shoulder and arm are fine, just bruised. They'll heal in a few days but they might get a little stiff. But until then, you won't want to pick up or hold a child. I can write an order for physical therapy on that arm, if you like?"

Thad stepped forward. "*Nein*, we don't

have money for that. Isn't there something she can do at home that I could help her with?"

"Of course. Just have her start with stretches, then in a day or two add light exercises like lifting a can or fruit jar. When the shoulder heals some, she can lift the can over her head to stretch out the muscles until she gets her strength back."

Her heart gave a cold shiver. "How many weeks will I need to do the exercises?"

The doctor glanced up from writing on the chart. "Keep them up until the shoulder and arm are totally healed, three, maybe four weeks until it's totally healed. Start the stretches right away. In a day or two start the exercises. Also," he pointed to an egg-shaped lump on the top of her foot, "that bone chip torpedoed up and into your muscle when it broke, causing tissue damage. That's why you have this swelling. Apply ice packs when you get home. Twenty minutes on and twenty minutes off for two hours and that should take the swelling down. Later today or tomorrow, dark bruising will spread over the top of the foot, but it'll go away. It will take about four to six weeks for that bone to heal."

She tamped down the nausea that threatened. Fear twisted her stomach into a knot. "Four to six weeks? I live on a farm. I can't be laid up that long."

"I'm sorry, but you don't want to do permanent damage to that foot."

"Still, with the restrictions, I'll need to hire a mother's helper."

"That shouldn't really be necessary, but suit yourself. Just no running, and stairs will be awkward to maneuver with the boot. For the next few days, you're going to be very sore and walking may be difficult until the swelling goes down."

May slumped back against Thad.

"May, don't worry. I'll help you. We'll work it all out together."

"I've heard that the Amish always helped each other out in times of need."

"*Jah*, we do." May nodded. "I just hate to impose on others. It's canning season and everyone's gardens are ready at once. But it can't be helped."

Dr. Kincaid placed May's foot in the walking boot and fastened the straps snugly around her foot and leg. "I want to see you in six weeks. In the meantime, remember, no work, stay off the foot and apply ice three times a day until the swelling is gone."

May thanked the doctor for his help while Thad left her for a moment to go call a driver to bring them home.

She slumped back in the chair next to Thad while they waited for their ride. A dark cloud pressed down on her as she thought about Leah. She'd be worried and confused when she awoke in the morning at the Brennemans and not in her own bed, in her own home with May snuggling her close.

"May, are you okay?" Thad reached over and lightly laid his hand on top of hers.

"*Jah*, just thinking about Leah. I hope she's not scared."

How was Leah ever going to handle this? *Nein.* How was she ever going to handle this?

Sixty minutes later, the SUV arrived at their farm. May clutched the sheet of instructions for her medicines, the care of her injured foot and her next appointment written at the top. As Thad ran around to her side of the car to help her out, she stared out the window at the porch steps. "I never noticed before, but there are so many steps."

"Don't worry, I'm here to help you." He held the car door as she slid out and gingerly stepped on the ground. "Are you okay?"

"*Jah,* but can I hold on to your arm until we get inside the *haus*? I'm still getting used to walking in this boot."

He closed the door and held his elbow out for her to grab. Her boot clunked on each step until they slowly reached the top.

She stopped, released his arm and heaved a sigh.

Thad slid his arm around her waist. "You okay?"

"Just needed to rest a second." She drew in a deep breath. "I can make it the rest of the way on my own now."

Thad took his arm away from her waist and opened the door. May stepped in, stopping just inside.

Gretchen's voice shattered the silence. "What's been going on in here? It looks like you two were fighting, broken dishes and the stool turned over. Shame on you both! Thad, you're too old to act like a hooligan. You never fought with April like this."

May's back stiffened. "We didn't have a disagreement." She hobbled to a chair and sat down feeling Gretchen's scalding glare on her back.

"I've cleaned up the mess you two made."

"*Mamm*, May fell off the stool putting away dishes and broke a bone in her foot.

Danki for cleaning up the mess. I had planned on doing that when we returned."

"Where is Leah?"

"I called Sarah and Caleb Brenneman and they came and got Leah. They will keep her a few nights until May is feeling better."

"You had me worried sick. I didn't know what was going on. You should have run over to the *dawdi haus* and told me."

"May was in a lot of pain, and I didn't want to leave her. I figured we'd be back before you even noticed."

"Of course I noticed. I worry about what goes on over here."

"*Danki*, Gretchen, I appreciate your concern. And *danki* for cleaning up the mess."

Thad stepped toward his *mamm*. "May isn't feeling well and I'm going to help her into bed. You can visit with her tomorrow."

He pressed a hand to his *mamm*'s back and escorted her swiftly to the door. "I'll let you know tomorrow how she is feeling."

Gretchen huffed and strutted out the door, as she headed back to the *dawdi haus*.

When Thad closed the door and turned, he shrugged. They both knew Thad's mother was a handful. "Are you going to pick up Leah at Sarah and Caleb's?"

"*Nein*, not for a few days. You're tired and need rest. Tomorrow, we'll talk about new arrangements for Leah and about hiring someone to take over your work."

"I'm worried about her."

"I know, but the Brennemans will take very *gut* care of her. Quit worrying. Right now, you think about yourself."

"I… I can take care of Leah just fine." A nervous laugh belied her words. Her arm and shoulder throbbed and her foot was so swollen she could hardly move it. But she was sure Thad saw through her ruse.

"*Nein*. You cannot. I don't want you hurting your foot any further or risk you dropping Leah. Maybe when the swelling is down and you're stable on your feet, but not now. You wobble like a pregnant cow ready to calve. Let's get you upstairs so you can rest and I'll bring you some ice for that foot." He helped her to stand up, placed his arm around her and gently supported her.

At the touch of his strong arm pulling her close, an unexpected spark of excitement coursed through her. Her traitorous heart raced as she tried to control it, to dismiss it like it hadn't happened. Only it had. She focused her attention to the staircase just ahead and tried to bring her breathing back to normal.

She took a step but swayed as the boot and swollen foot interrupted her balance for a second.

She hadn't realized just how much strength the ordeal had sapped from her. Her head began to pound. She gulped a breath and tried to flash Thad a smile, but no doubt he could see through her efforts.

She was sure pain, worry and weakness etched lines around her eyes.

Thad shook his head. "*Nein*, I've made

the decision, you are too weak right now to take care of Leah. I'll see if I can hire a mother's helper. Do you know of a girl who might take the job for a couple of months, or for at least the next two or three weeks? We'll need her to live here."

May thought for a moment. "My cousin Josie. She is the only one I can think of." Fear edged into her throat as her voice shook the last sentence into existence. She loved her cousin but she was as bossy as *Aent* Matilda.

Thad noticed the strained expression on May's face as she sat on her bed, and he couldn't decide if it was from physical pain or the pain of missing Leah. He patted her back. "Is there anything you need right now?"

She pushed his hand away. "I'm fine. I can take care of myself."

From what he'd seen, that didn't seem to be the case, but he let it go for now.

May rubbed her free hand over her injured right arm. "I could rest for a while, and then we could go over and see how Leah is doing."

"*Nein.* Let's not confuse her any more than she probably already is with staying with them. To visit her and leave would just upset her. When they picked up Leah, Sarah said since she is expecting her first *boppli*, she's anxious to have Leah around for the experience and to get her household in a routine of helping with a wee one."

He walked to the door, glanced back and caught the lonely expression that crossed May's face. She spent every waking hour with Leah. He could see it was upsetting for her to let her pumpkin stay somewhere else just a few nights, not to mention a week or more. "I'll offer Josie a little more if she'll come right away."

"*Danki*, Thad."

He couldn't tell by the sound of her voice if she was feeling relief or dread. "I'll call her right away."

"*Aent* Matilda's number is on the pad in the barn."

He nodded. "I won't be a minute."

Thad hurried to the barn and the phone that the bishop had allowed him to have ever since April was pregnant and went long overdue. He'd used it to call the emergency unit when April died after she delivered the baby.

He swallowed back that memory and dialed the number of the phone shanty by May's *Aent* Matilda. He explained their dilemma and asked if Josie would be available to come and stay a few weeks. He left his number and hung up.

Since May was napping, he strolled to the north forty to check on the *youngies* and see if they had completed weeding the field. Carl was supervising the others. As he approached, it looked like Carl had everything under control. The field looked clean. He waved and Carl ran between two rows to where he was standing.

"How's it going, Carl?"

"Real *gut*. We're almost done."

"We'll pick on Friday. Will you tell the other *buwe*?"

"Sure, no problem. Ethan has gone to the barn to start the milking process. When we get done here, would you like us to go help him?"

"*Jah*, that would be *gut*."

"How's May?"

He shook his head. "Her foot really hurts and doc said it would be a few weeks to heal but she is in a boot and getting around for the most part."

"That's *wunderbaar*."

Thad headed back to the barn and as he got close, he heard the phone ringing, which set his feet to hard run. He yanked open the door, and got the phone just in time.

"I almost hung up." Josie chuckled. "I was just planning on leaving a message. I can't come right away. I have other commitments and can't come until a week from today, is that okay?"

"*Jah*, that'll work. *Danki*."

Thad panted, trying to get his breath back as he entered the kitchen. May would probably be awake, stewing about where he was and if he heard back from Josie.

He tapped lightly on her door in case she was asleep, then edged the door open and stuck his head around the corner.

"I'm awake."

"How do you feel? But that's probably a stupid question."

"I feel a little better. Why are you panting?"

He took a deep breath and blew it out. "Sorry, I ran to the *haus* from the barn. Josie can't come for a week, so we'll need to let Sarah and Caleb take care of Leah until Josie can make it."

It was the first smile he'd seen on her face since he'd broken May's heart. "Why the smile?"

"I was afraid that Josie might have gotten another job and wouldn't be able to make it. That's a big load off my mind knowing that Leah can come home in a few days."

Leah was her ray of sunshine. He hoped someday he could put a smile like that back on her face. "I'll make you a cup of tea."

May gave him a thankful nod, her eyes brimming with softness like clear, turquoise ocean water covering a warm sandy beach. It was funny how that image just flashed through his mind. One day when they were courting, May confided how she wanted to see the ocean wash up on a beach. She wanted to walk through the surf with her bare feet and let the wet sand squish between her toes.

When the teakettle whistled, he put a tea bag in each cup and poured in hot water. He put a few cookies on the tray and carried it upstairs. He pulled a chair up by the bed and set the tray on her lap. He swirled the bag around in his cup, eventually pulling it out and setting it on the tea bag holder sitting on the tray.

He glanced over at May, still swirling her bag. "You must like strong tea."

"What?" She looked up, then back down at her tea. "Not really." She tugged the bag from the cup and set it next to his. She gingerly put the cup to her lips and took a sip as her eyes stared at the quilt.

"Something bothering you, May?"

"I just keep thinking about Leah. She'll miss me."

"Sarah and Caleb's son Jacob will entertain her, and their daughter Mary will fuss over her, no doubt. She'll *liebe* it there."

"That's what I'm worried about. I'll seem like dull company when she comes home."

"What? Don't be ridiculous! You're her *mamm*. She will always *liebe* you. Maybe we should get her a kitten or dog to play with. No doubt Jacob will introduce her to his cat, Tiger."

May wrinkled her nose. "We'll see. She's only a year old. Maybe later."

"I know you miss her. Whenever you want

to see Leah, and you're feeling strong enough, I'll take you to the Brenneman's *haus*."

Her face brightened. *"Danki."*

"Now, you look tired and need to rest. I'm going to check the refrigerator. Was there any ribs left over?"

May jerked her head in his direction. *"Nein,* but I don't think I can make supper."

He nodded. "I'll fry some ham and make us French toast, how does that sound?"

"Great. I'm going to take a nap." She picked the tray up off her lap and handed it to him.

"Do you want to eat downstairs? I can come up and get you."

"The swelling in my foot is down. I think I can manage."

"I'm going to make sure. I'll come up and help you. You are too important of a commodity to have anything happen to you."

She smiled for the second time today.

"You're too late, I'm already damaged goods." She pointed to her foot.

He gave her a wink as he stood. "*Jah*, but now you are captive company."

After chores, Thad washed up, sliced the ham and then made the batter for French toast. The sizzling maple-glazed ham permeated the air with an aroma that teased his stomach.

Thump. Thump.

He stepped back from the stove and listened. *Thump.* He sat his spatula down on the spoon rest and ran to the stairs. "I thought you were going to wait until I came and helped you?"

"I wanted to see if I could maneuver this boot around." Under his cautious eye, May shuffled through the door and slumped into a chair at the table. "Mmm, that smells *gut*. I didn't know I was so hungry."

"I'm glad you're not too picky. My skills as a cook are limited, I'm afraid."

"*Nein*. I'm very grateful to you for all

your help. You know your *mamm* wouldn't approve if she saw you waving that spatula like you know what you're doing."

Thad grinned. "What she doesn't know won't hurt her. When I was young and hungry and *Mamm* wasn't home, I cooked all the time." He raised his spatula up and down in the air as if he was lifting a hundred-pound bale of hay.

"*Ach*, my hero," she laughed, and their eyes met for a second before she pulled away.

A soft knock sounded on the door. Thad put down his spatula. "I hope it's not *Mamm* again," he whispered as he passed May.

He opened the door to three wonderful women holding baskets of what smelled like food. "Come in, come in. And if that is what I think it is, I can retire my spatula for a few days."

Hannah Smith, Minnie Miller and Mary Brenneman, her neighbors and dear friends, crowded through the door, laughing at

Thad and rushing to May's side. They each swirled an arm around May and hugged her gently.

"We were so sorry to hear about your fall." Hannah set her basket of food on the table. "There's a couple casseroles here, plus breads, meat loaf and desserts. You— or Thad—won't have to cook for several days."

"*Danki*, that's *wunderbaar.*"

"So how is married life treating you?" Minnie asked, with a teasing tone. "Maybe we shouldn't ask since you broke your foot and you'll be chained to this *haus* for several days."

The ladies chatted, sharing the latest news of Jesse and Kim Kauffman, who were moving to Indiana, and Turner and Naomi Lapp were expecting another *boppli*. They teased May and Thad a little before saying good-night and then headed home, promising they would be back soon to visit.

Thad closed the door after them. "Supper is almost cold."

"That's okay. I'm starved. You made it, and I'm going to eat it."

Something in the way May said that warmed his heart. It had a pleasant tone and even a fondness. Could it be that she was finally setting the past on the shelf and going to give their marriage a chance?

Chapter Seven

A golden stream of sunbeams poured through May's window and warmed her face. Reluctantly her eyes opened. She glanced at the clock. 10:00 a.m. She'd slept all through the night and almost all morning. She had slept for twelve hours. Thad would think her lazy.

She jerked upright, then stopped. A wave of pain seized her foot, and a pronounced ache traveled from her shoulder down her back to her hips. It was as if a horse and buggy had driven over her. She threw her legs over the side of the bed, stepped into her ankle brace and stood. Another wave of pain washed over her. She moved slowly toward the hook where her dress hung on the wall.

Each step was a challenge. She stopped, pulled in a deep breath and blew it out.

Her muscles felt tight and needed stretching. The fall yesterday must have pulled and bruised every muscle in her body. She rested for a moment, then sucked in three deep breaths and walked to the wall where a peg held her dress. She pulled her dress off the peg, draped it over her head and slipped her injured arm through the sleeve, then the other. *Ach*, it hurt more than she thought it would. She bit her lip and braced her back against the wall for a moment. She felt a little dizzy from the pain. In a minute, it cleared.

A soft tap sounded on the bedroom door.

"Yes. Is that you, Thad?"

The door cracked open. "Can I come in a minute?"

"Stay right there. I don't have my prayer *kapp* on." Her hair was a mess. She couldn't let him see her like this, and she probably needed to pinch her cheeks and bring a little color to them.

"Caleb called while I was in the barn. They will bring Leah back to us next Friday, if we decide that you're feeling better and ready to handle her."

"That would be *wunderbaar.*"

"Do you need help getting dressed?" His voice seemed hesitant.

"*Nein.* I'm just sore and moving slow as a caterpillar. I'll be down in a minute to fix breakfast."

"Not necessary. I've already fixed scrambled eggs and sliced ham. So when you come down, it'll be waiting for you."

Had she heard him right? She pushed away from the wall and took a step in his direction. "You made breakfast?"

He chuckled. "Don't be so surprised. I told you last night, just because I'm a man doesn't mean I don't know how to cook a little or take care of myself. I'm heading back out. I left a note on the table, but I wanted to check on you. I'll stop back later." He pulled the door closed.

She smiled.

A small spark of relief surged through her as she fought with her prayer *kapp* to get it in place over her bun. The next time Sarah or someone stopped by, she'd ask them to help her with her hair. She sighed at the effort it took to get dressed. It would have been noon before she had breakfast ready, moving at this pace.

The aroma of strong coffee hit May's nostrils when she entered the kitchen, followed by the tantalizing whiff of honey-glazed ham that set her stomach growling. She reached for the orange juice in the gas-powered refrigerator and gasped at what she saw. Thad had made meat loaf sandwiches, all wrapped up and stacked on a shelf ready for lunch.

A tinge of guilt nudged her. He was trying to be nice, and she appreciated that.

A smile pulled at the corner of her mouth although she tried to resist. For sure and certain, he had a sweet way about him sometimes.

A knock sounded on the screen door, then it opened. "*Ach*, Janie, what are you doing? Come in, come in."

Janie rushed to May and gave her a big hug. "It's all over town that you fell and some big handsome man caught you and saved your life. That big strong man wouldn't happen to be your *wunderbaar ehemann*, would it?" She gave her a knowing wink.

"He didn't exactly catch me. I wish he would have, then I might not have broken my foot. *Danki* for stopping by."

"Of course. I baked you some cookies. Chocolate chip." Janie held up a plate covered with plastic wrap. "What else would you like help with while I'm here?"

"Could you help me wash my hair? My arm and shoulder are sore and it's hard to lift my arms above my head."

"I can do that while I tell you my big news. Let's go to the sink. Where's your shampoo?"

"Under the sink. *Ach*, what big news?"

Janie giggled. "Jonah Hochstetler asked me out."

"Nein," May gasped.

"Yes, yes, yes. He is every bit as handsome as his big brother Thad."

"When did all this happen?"

"At the wedding while you were busy being a new *frau*. We spent most of the afternoon together."

"I can't believe you waited so long to tell me."

"Now, May, as you well know, courting is a private matter to the Amish. Besides, I wanted to make sure there was some kind of spark. Some real feelings there. *Ach*, then he asked me out again." She gave a little scream, then quieted. "I hope Gretchen the Grouch didn't hear me."

May smiled behind her hand. Her mother-in-law was rather grouchy. But it wasn't right to agree with Janie openly. "So how many times have you gone out with him?"

"Several times. It's been so *wunderbaar.* I really like him, May. I was hoping that Simon would ask Josie out, but it didn't happen. I think she sort of liked him."

"For real? I hadn't noticed any of this going on at my wedding."

"*Jah*, well, you were a little busy with that handsome *ehemann* of yours. Don't think I didn't notice you two holding hands and snuggling at times."

"Oh, stop. He just had his arm around me, and he is my *ehemann* after all."

"I know. I just wanted to see if you did, too. How are you two getting along in your bargain marriage?"

"I shouldn't have told you about that. You must never tell anyone. Promise me, Janie."

"May, anyone could figure it out. You hated him something awful after he married April. I'm actually shocked you gave in to the bishop."

May shot Janie a stern stare. "I had my reasons."

"How does your hair feel? It's all clean and back up in a bun."

"I forgot to tell you, Josie is coming to stay a few weeks and help me take care of Leah while my foot is healing. If she likes him so much, maybe we could have Simon over for dinner."

"Now, May, don't go playing match-maker. You didn't like it when the bishop first came to you."

"That was different. I'm only going to ask him if he is interested."

Janie chatted away, listing all the pros and cons to a match between Simon and Josie. "If it did happen, and she married Simon and I married Jonah, we would all three be sisters. *Ach*, that would be *wunderbaar*. *Jah*, and now before I go, I'm going to tidy up Thad's messy kitchen." Janie cleaned the stove and washed dishes, the whole time talking and sharing her dream for her and Jonah.

May smiled and got a word in sideways occasionally.

Thad had cooked breakfast. He was good to make eggs and sandwiches, even though he hadn't cleaned up.

She was grateful to Thad, and to Janie, for all the help around the house. But a veil of shame covered May's heart. She was careless to have gotten up on the stool and fallen. Now Thad had to spend his valuable time helping her, or paying others to do her work. Josie would work for free, but she knew Thad would want to pay her. Money he didn't have right now. She felt useless. Instead of helping Thad, she was a burden to him.

The week passed slowly. May rested as much as possible to keep the swelling down. She scratched around the boot. Her foot was already mending. She could feel it getting stronger every day. The bruising was gone.

She puttered around the kitchen. When she opened a cupboard door, she noticed Thad had rearranged the contents so the dishes they used every day were more accessible on the lower shelves. It was nice how he surprised her with these little helpful gestures without asking her, just taking it upon himself to make things more convenient.

She smiled to herself when she thought of him working in the kitchen, and an image of him with his beard tickled her memory. When they courted, he was single and clean-shaven, but Old Order Amish followed the law Moses gave that a man at adulthood wasn't to cut his hair or beard. But May didn't mind. The beard matured his face and even gave him a dignified appearance. With some men, the beard changed their appearance, and it wasn't for the better. She couldn't say that about

Thad. His dark hair and beard framed his dark blue eyes.

When he was in the *haus* with her, his gaze often followed her when he thought she wasn't looking. He wanted to help her, but she had to show him she was strong enough to take care of Leah.

May scooped up a dust cloth. She worked alone for two hours, dusting and cleaning until her good arm started to tire. But it was important she show Thad she was getting stronger and ready to have Leah come back home. She straightened her back and stretched to ease the tightness. Today, her arm was only a little sore but felt stronger. Her foot felt comfortable in the boot. Tonight, a nice dose of liniment smoothed over the foot and arm would help them heal even faster.

She glanced at the clock. Almost noon. May opened the refrigerator and pulled out the sandwiches she had noticed earlier that Thad must have made again, poured the lemonade and set the plates on the table.

At noon, she heard Thad's boots thumping up the porch steps and the screen door squeak open. He hesitated when he saw her and jerked his head toward the table. "How are you feeling today?" he drawled in Pennsylvania Dutch.

"A little better. *Danki* for rearranging the cupboards." It amazed her how simply that gratitude rolled off her tongue, with no bitter undertone.

Thad must have noticed, because his bunched shoulders relaxed as he washed up at the sink, then he took an easy gait to his chair at the table.

A playful smile pulled at the corners of his mouth for the briefest second before he wiped it away. She could see he wanted to make another comment but thought he'd better not tempt the light mood.

After silent prayer, May took a bite of her meat loaf sandwich. It actually felt *gut* to eat a sandwich that Thad had made especially for her.

A knock sounded and the screen door opened. "Yoo-hoo! Is anyone home?"

May's back stiffened.

Thad called out, "Come in, *Mamm*."

"*Hullo*, dear. I came to see how May was doing and if there was anything I could do to help."

"That was very nice of you to stop by, *Mamm*, but we have everything under control."

May threw Thad a sidelong look. She liked his vote of confidence. "*Danki* for stopping by, Gretchen. I'm doing much better and up on my feet. It is a little slow going in the boot, but I'm managing." Hopefully, this was Gretchen's way of trying to make amends.

"Well, if you don't need any help right now, I'll stop by again tomorrow."

May and Thad finished their lunch, and Thad set his napkin down on the kitchen table.

"I have a dairy association meeting at four

o'clock this afternoon. Will you be okay staying here by yourself for a little while?"

"Of course, but could you lift that bucket of string beans to the table so I can snap them?"

May grabbed a towel and laid it on the table, and he set the bucket down. "I'll stick my head back in before I go. Anything else?"

"*Nein*, I'm *gut*."

After an hour of snapping beans, she stretched and exercised her arm, then finished snapping the beans. She rinsed the beans in cold water, drained and stored the bowls in the refrigerator.

Thad poked his head in the door and called out. "May, I'm leaving for the meeting."

"Fine. See you later."

She had just enough time to rest, then she'd have to start thinking about supper, although that would be easy. So many members of their community had dropped off food. May laid her head against the back of the chair in the living room for just a minute to rest.

Sometime later, she heard someone call her name. "May. May?"

She opened her eyes and noticed her *ehemann* standing over her, the sweet smell of the goat's milk soap wafting in the air. "Oh, you're home. How was the meeting?"

"Not *gut*." He sat down next to her. "Because there is an overproduction of organic milk, the association is only selling 85 percent and the rest is being sold at regular price. This is on top of the price of the organic milk dropping, too."

May gasped. She reached over and covered his hand with hers. "How long can we last with just the crops for income?"

He leaned his head on the back of the chair, then lifted it and faced her. "Not long. The only way we are surviving this year is because of our vegetable crop. Let's pray we don't have weather that will ruin it. But if the dairy association can't get a response from the USDA, we might have to take drastic action."

"What kind of action?" Panic swept through her.

"Sell out!"

Fear prickled the hair on her arm as her gaze met his. Besides Leah, saving the farm was the reason she made the marriage bargain. Selling wasn't going to happen.

Nein, not if she had to sell every stick of furniture they had, she wouldn't let them lose the farm.

Chapter Eight

May stood at the kitchen sink while the Friday morning sun streamed in through the window onto the African violet sitting on the windowsill. She checked the plant's soil. *Jah*, still moist.

Her thoughts wandered to the farm. What could she do to bring in a significant amount of money? Get a job? Who would take care of Leah? *Nein*, she'd miss her pumpkin too much to get a job.

Hearing buggy wheels and horse's hooves clomping up the drive, she glanced out the window, hurried across the porch and clunked her boot down each step.

Thad raced from the barn and they reached Sarah and Caleb's carriage at the same time.

Caleb helped Sarah and Leah down, and as soon as Leah saw May, she nearly jumped into her arms.

"*Mamm*. Home, *Mamm*."

"I'm so glad you're here, sweetheart. *Danki* for taking care of her."

Sarah gave a flip of her hand to wave the thought away. "We were glad to do it. We loved having her. She missed you, but Jacob and Mary kept her busy and entertained."

She hugged Leah as her arms encircled May's neck. She kissed her pumpkin's cheek. "It's so *gut* to have you home. I have missed you."

Seven-year-old Jacob lifted a box from the carriage and set it on the ground. "*Jah*, I can carry her easy."

"*Jah?* You must be very strong." May winked.

"She even has a loud burp, louder than my *boppli bu* cousin."

"Jacob. A gentleman doesn't tattle on a lady." Caleb smiled. "She was the perfect *haus* guest. We will watch her any time you want us to."

Thad put his arms around both Leah and May and gave a hug. Leah turned to her *daed* and planted a big kiss on his cheek. "*Danki*, Leah, I missed you, too. Come in the *haus*, all of you. I'm sure May has some coffee she could brew."

While Caleb pulled Leah's crib mattress from his buggy, Thad and Jacob carried in the rest of her things and toted them straight up to her room.

May headed to the stove. "The coffee is hot. Would you like a cup, Sarah?"

"*Nein*, we have other errands to run and thought we'd drop her off first. I knew you'd be anxious to see her."

The men tromped down the stairs and returned to the kitchen.

"Come on, Jacob, time to go." Caleb headed for the door, held it open and motioned for Sarah to go before him.

Sarah turned back toward May. "Let me know if you need any more help. We'll be glad to watch Leah again."

"*Danki* for everything."

Thad came back in the kitchen from seeing them off. He walked over to May, and kissed his *tochter* on the cheek. Leah reached her arms out to her *daed*. "Oh, so you are going to come and see me. I was feeling bad that May was the only special one." He glanced at May.

"*Jah*, she loves her *daed*."

"I have a surprise for you, Leah. Mama cow has a new baby. Shall we go see it?"

Leah nodded.

"Want to come, May?"

"*Nein*, not right now. You spend time with your *tochter* alone."

May unpacked Leah's boxes of bottles. Filled them and placed them in the refrigerator.

The slamming of a car door pulled her gaze to the window. She hurried to the door and pushed it open. Her cousin stepped out of the car, as the driver lifted her luggage out of the trunk. She paid him and dragged her suitcase to the porch.

"*Ach*, Josie, how nice to see you. *Danki* for coming."

"It's no problem, I wanted to help. How are you feeling?" She gave May a hug.

"Would you like a cup of coffee?"

"*Nein*, sit. I'm here to help you."

"*Danki*, but I'm getting along much better." May started toward the cupboard. "I'll probably just need your help a couple of weeks or so."

The screen door banged as Thad stepped inside with Leah in his arms. He set Leah on the floor with her toys, then bent down to pick up Josie's suitcase. "As long as she is here and ready to stay a few days, we will accept her offer of assistance. Leah and I just went out to the pasture to see a new baby calf."

Josie smiled and looked at Leah. "*Hullo*, sweet girl. Did you go out and see the baby calf?"

Leah squealed and pointed her finger. "Did you see mama cow, too?"

Leah jabbered on and on, laughing and giggling, then jabbered more about her adventure.

Josie glanced at Thad. "You are a very popular *daed* right now."

He motioned to the door. "*Danki* for coming, Josie. I'll take your suitcase upstairs so you can get settled in your room."

Thad tossed May a what-are-you-doing look with a raised brow. She raised her brow right back at him. She knew his concerns. She'd told Josie she didn't need to stay too long, and he wanted to make sure May had all the help she needed.

She shrugged, picked up Leah and laid her in her downstairs crib for a nap. She followed Thad and Josie to make sure Josie was comfortable with the room.

Thad had plunked the suitcase down on the bed and gave May a cautionary look. "I'm glad you're here, Josie. May really needs the help. She needs to stay off that foot or it will never heal." His tone carried a note of concern.

"We're fine. Go do the chores. Supper will be ready when you're done." May rewarded his thoughtfulness with a gentle smile. "I can be on the foot. I just need to rest, too."

"*Danki* for coming, Josie." Thad got the last word in. When they'd courted long ago, she had thought *Gott* had handpicked Thad for her. Who knew? Maybe this had been God's purpose and plan for her all along.

Thad heaved a sigh as he unhitched Honeydew, and laid the collar and breeching off to the side. An image of May looking fetching today fought its way back into his mind. Her cheeks had a glow that he hadn't seen in a long time. Had Josie's visit put it there?

He brushed the horse down, hooked a fresh bucket of oats on the fence and closed the gate. He had hoped that eventually May would forgive him for the past, and it seemed like she had started to do just that. He just hoped and prayed that she never found out the true reason he'd married April or she'd never forgive him. Never.

Thad finished his chores and made his way back across the barnyard to the *haus*. It bothered him that he'd lied to May, or rather, that he hadn't told her the whole truth, but he knew it was for her own *gut*. He shuddered to think what she would say or do if she knew he had lied to her. To everyone. If she ever found out, this little bit of heaven with her that he'd found would be over.

He approached the driveway, looked up and saw a buggy there. *Nein*... It was Elmer's horse and buggy nearly blocking his way. What was he doing here?

His stomach twisted into a knot as he opened the door to the aroma of baked ham, gravy and biscuits swirling through the air around him.

May gestured him to the sink to wash up. "*Gut*, you're here. We are ready to sit down."

Thad nodded. "Evening, Elmer."

Elmer nodded back. "It is indeed, Thad. I thought there for a minute you were going to leave me with these two ladies to enjoy their company by myself."

He raised a brow. "Not a chance."

Back when May had turned sixteen, Elmer had told Thad he wanted to ask May if he could court her. Thad had known that his brother Alvin and April would drop May off at the singing, so Thad ran over and asked May out first. He had done it to spite Elmer, not because he had any real interest in May. Since they were *buwe*, he and Elmer had always had a rivalry. They competed over everything. Who had the best horse, the nicest buggy, took the prettiest girl home from the singing.

Elmer was plenty miffed at him when he asked first to court May. But he unintentionally led May to believe he cared about her. He did like her, but not true love. At least, he didn't think he was in *liebe* with her. After Thad married April, Elmer had made it known what he thought of Thad for hurting May. He knew then how much Elmer cared for May.

Sitting down at the opposite end of the table from May, Thad bowed his head for silent prayer.

Moments later, he tapped the fork against his plate, then speared a piece of chicken from the platter sitting in front of him. "So, Elmer, how is the cheese business?"

"*Gut.* Since they invited our cheese factory to join the Iowa Cheese Club and the Iowa Cheese Roundup, business has been booming. The artisanal cheese flavors that we developed at Sunnyhill Cheese Factory are popular. The bacon and dried tomato flavors are our two favorites. Now, we ship cheese to people all over the world."

"That's impressive. I'm glad to hear it." Thad nodded as he took a bite of food.

Elmer glanced across the table at Josie.

"So you're May's cousin? I don't believe we've ever met before, or I would have remembered you. You and May look so much alike, you could be sisters." His mouth opened as if he had something more to say, but he closed it again.

"May, have you ever been to Elmer's cheese factory?" Josie asked pointedly.

May sat her fork down and glanced at Elmer, then at Josie. "Not for a long time. I'm probably way past due for a visit. Would you like to go sometime?"

"*Jah.* Maybe Elmer will show us around." Josie smiled at him.

"I'd be delighted. How about Monday?" His gaze bounced from Josie to May. "I'll be expecting you both then."

Thad liked the idea of Josie's sudden interest in Elmer. Maybe then Elmer would go over to her *haus* to visit instead of parking his buggy in his driveway.

"And, May, dear," Josie interjected, "if you get tired, you can sit and rest while Elmer shows me around the factory."

Thad glanced at May's face. She was smiling, which told him that she might have the same idea as he did about Elmer and Josie. In fact, perhaps she was even matchmaking at this very moment.

Only time would tell.

On Monday, May asked Thad to hitch up Gumdrop to the buggy for their trip to the cheese factory.

"Sure you don't want me to hitch Honeydew instead? He's big, but gentle."

"No, *danki*. I appreciate the offer." She gave him a wry look. "Gumdrop needs the exercise. And besides, I might be in a hurry on the way home and want a younger, faster horse."

"I'll have the buggy at the door in a few minutes." A chuckle followed his words.

Josie talked nonstop the whole way over to Sunnyhill Cheese Factory about Elmer—he was nice, handsome, caring, etc., etc., etc. May nodded in response but hoped Josie didn't talk nonstop on the tour.

Elmer was waiting when they pulled in the drive and helped them down from the buggy. "I cleared my schedule so I could show you around this morning."

He escorted them to his office, where May left the *boppli* bag and tied Leah to Josie's back. That way, she could sleep and wouldn't be so hard to carry. Elmer started the tour by taking them to a large white building.

After pointing out the different areas first, he started explaining the process from the beginning, with the arrival of the milk. He showed the fresh, foamy milk, supplied by the surrounding small-herd Amish farmers, pouring into a large vat. He waved his arm at the large sign that read:

Sunnyhill uses only organic milk from Amish farmers' pasture-fed cows.

May tried to linger behind them as much as possible to give Josie and Elmer time alone to get acquainted. *Jah*, she was going to make sure Josie was the first thing he saw every time he turned around. She hoped it worked out between them. They were both special to May and they deserved happiness.

Elmer showed them the process for making cheese, then explained the ripening process. He took them into the aging room so they could see the large wheels of cheese stacked on shelves all the way to the ceiling. May surveyed the huge amount of cheese that Elmer had stacked and aged that would bring him in money months from now.

Josie stood next to Elmer. Very close, in fact. "I have never seen so much cheese before. It's definitely macaroni and cheese for supper tonight."

"I'll happily supply the cheese," Elmer volunteered, "so you can see how *gut* the cheese is that we make."

"*Nein*, Elmer." May shook her head. "I've been here before and bought your cheese. You don't need to give us any." She tried to keep the tease out of her voice and make it sound serious.

"But I'm anxious for Josie to try it. Then she can come back and tell me how she liked it."

Josie beamed. "*Jah*, I'll do that."

"While you two finish the tour, I need to change a diaper. I'll wait for you in Elmer's office." She untied Leah from Josie's back, turned to leave and caught Josie batting her eyes at Elmer. "Don't be long, Josie."

She guessed Elmer wouldn't be stopping by the house to help her out any more. Not that he ever really did, except for the time Thad requested he help him fix the swollen doors.

At the time, she'd been angry with Thad for disturbing them. Farm life could be lonely, and it was nice when Elmer paid a visit. Yet she'd known that at some point she'd have to tell Elmer she wouldn't marry him. Now it appeared Josie had set her sights on him. So that was one task stricken from her to-do list.

May sat Leah upright and she smiled and pointed here, then over there, then somewhere else. "So many new sights in Elmer's office for little eyes, huh?"

Leah smiled as if it was some fun game to play. May picked her up and snuggled her close.

"What are you telling me, sweetheart, some really big story about the cheese factory?" May tickled Leah's tummy.

She giggled. "Stop, *Mamm*." She pulled herself up on the back of the couch and gave May a toothy smile.

Josie hurried into the office. "Elmer is bringing our buggy to the door. I've asked him to come to dinner tonight." She held out a big brick of cheese. "I promised I would make macaroni and cheese for him with this. What do you think?"

"I think if you are cooking, then that is a terrific idea. So are there sparks flying between you two?" May stuffed Leah's things back into her bag and handed it to Josie. "Do you mind carrying this? My leg is tired from lugging this boot around, and I don't want to fall. That's all I need, another injury."

Josie led the way to the buggy. "We're just friends, Elmer and I," she said, shooting May a coy look. "For now anyway."

After Elmer brought the buggy around and helped them up into it, May shook the reins and Gumdrop took off with a jerk, but soon settled into an even trot. Before they were out of the drive and past the big buildings, Leah was fast asleep.

May glanced at Josie, who was staring out the window. Her cousin looked deep in thought worrying her bottom lip. "Something wrong, Josie?"

"*Nein.* Do you think Elmer is courting anyone?"

There it was. May had wondered when Josie would get around to asking that question and how she should answer. In the Amish community, courting was a private affair and not talked about, and folks never knew who was courting who until the reading of the banns at church.

Elmer had never officially asked May if he could court her, but at times when she was single, she thought he might. Yet that seemed like it was ages ago, and today, on the cheese tour, she was sure she'd seen Elmer stare at Josie.

May felt Josie's stare, waiting for an answer. "You know courting is a private matter. He has not mentioned anything to me, so I don't have the answer for you. I'm sorry, Josie."

"*Gut*. I'm going to take that as *nein*." Josie settled back in the seat and crossed her arms.

Josie talked a lot and Elmer had his quiet moments; they would be a *gut* match.

If that was true, was it also true that the bishop saw some qualities that were compatible between her and Thad? That he at times seemed resigned to give up the farm but she had a spark of energy that could get them through these hard times.

And just like that, she knew how to save the farm...

Chapter Nine

At the end of his long workday, Thad crossed the barnyard toward the *haus*, sweat running down his face and trickling down his back. He'd sleep *gut* tonight. His pace slowed as he approached the *haus*. A spanking-clean buggy sat in the drive. *Elmer.* Was he here courting Josie?

He climbed the porch steps and paused for a second before opening the door. Elmer's deep voice had said something he didn't catch. May and Josie both laughed. Did the man ever work? Thad blew out a breath, plopped his hat on the wall peg, then washed his hands at the metal basin in the sink in the kitchen.

May hurried into the kitchen from the sitting room and began uncovering serving bowls and setting them on the table. "Thad, you look tired and hungry. Dinner will be on the table in a minute. Sit down."

"How is your foot after walking on it for the factory tour?"

"*Gut*, but I'm a little tired."

Thad looked Elmer up and down as he made his way to the table. There were no cheese curds on his clothes. He'd cleaned up for his visit. "Not busy at work today, Elmer?"

"On the contrary, business is booming. Tour buses come in every weekend. I had to hire more help. Mondays are slower, and it's the day I usually catch up on paperwork, but I reserved this morning for May and Josie's tour."

Thad nodded. *Tour buses.*

Josie helped set the food on the table, then sat across from Elmer. "He gave us a *wunderbaar* tour and a brick of cheese, so we're having mac and cheese for supper along with the pork chops."

"My favorite." Thad's voice went a little flat with fatigue stretching across his shoulders and down his back. He bowed his head for prayer, then silence swept over the room.

Thad listened to Josie go on and on about their visit to Sunnyhill Cheese Factory. Her face glowed as she spoke about his operation. The way Elmer looked back at Josie, Thad was sure he was only waiting until he knew her well enough to ask to court her.

Thad's heart thumped against his chest as he watched Elmer talk to May and smile at her. The three of them laughed and enjoyed reminiscing about the morning they'd shared together at the factory.

"Thad?"

He jerked his head to the other side. "I'm sorry, Josie, did you say something? I'm so tired even my ears are sleeping." Everyone chuckled at his joke.

"What do you think of the macaroni and cheese? I made it with cheese from Sunny-hill." Josie looked earnestly at Thad, waiting for an answer.

The three sets of eyes and ears at the table were not going to let him off without hearing his opinion. "It was very tasty. Maybe the best I've ever had."

After Josie and May heaped mountains of praise on Elmer's cheese, they finally expanded their conversation to other wonderful dishes that could benefit by Elmer's prize-winning cheese.

"Elmer, what do you say to one day we take these ladies on the Cheese Roundup? It could be a fun outing. We could hire a car." Thad picked up the bowl and piled more mac and cheese on his plate.

"What is the Cheese Roundup?" Josie glanced toward Thad, then back to Elmer. "I've heard of it but not quite sure what it is."

"That would be a *wunderbaar* time." Elmer nodded. "It's a mapped trail around Iowa that hits all the cheese factories. Along the trail are other places to visit like state parks and the Amana Colonies. It goes through Des Moines, Iowa City, Cedar Rapids, with all kinds of things to do. And there are lots of fun places to stay—lodges, inns and campgrounds. Of course, we wouldn't be gone that long, but cheese-tastings have been paired with all kinds of other events and festivals, so the customers can take a vacation, along with visiting the factories and shops."

"But if you want me to tag along," Thad pointed his fork at himself, "we'd need to go on a late fall day when harvesting was over."

May's head snapped his way. "We could take Leah. She'd love it."

"*Nein.* That would be too much for her, and it would give us time away together."

"I could carry her on my back, and she'll sleep while we walk."

"May, that would be too much for you and her. We'll think about it. We're not going tomorrow." The more he thought about time away and alone with May, the more he liked the idea.

"Well, I want to go," Josie cut in, already starting to plan the trip. She glanced in Thad's direction occasionally, and he nodded when appropriate. While they hashed it all over, he listened.

He glanced out the window. Still daylight. "If you'll excuse me, I have a few more chores to finish up. Always *gut* to see you, Elmer."

Thad retrieved his hat from the peg, tromped down the steps and headed to the shed. *Jah*, if he never heard any more about cheese or cheese factories, he'd be a happy man.

Queasiness roiled his stomach. Thad pulled the scythe and sickle from their hooks, carried them to the sharpening stone and sharpened their blades until they sliced through a piece of straw without resistance. Tomorrow, he'd work out his frustration on barnyard weeds.

He heard cows pushing against the barn door, bellowing in impatience, wanting to be milked. He'd lost track of time. Hurrying to hang the scythe and sickle back on their hooks, he washed and gloved his hands.

The barn door creaked open and Ethan's head appeared in the crack. "Need help with the milking, Mr. Hochstetler?"

"Perfect timing, Ethan. *Jah*, I got busy with other tasks and fell behind. Help me lead the Holsteins into the stanchions. I'll apply the iodine mixture to the udders, and you can follow behind with the alcohol wipe."

"Sounds *gut*. Do you want me to get a couple of the other guys to help so it goes faster?"

"*Danki, gut* idea." Thad blew out a long breath. His *onkel* Edward once told him idle thoughts were the devil's work and busy hands were *Gott*'s antidote.

He needed to wipe his jealousy from his head and from his heart. This was the perfect remedy.

May stood. "You two sit and visit. I'm going to clear the dessert plates off the table." She returned to refill Josie and Elmer's coffee cups.

Gathering the leftover bread from their meal, she threw it out on the lawn for the birds to nibble on. She glanced over at Thad's horse and buggy sitting in the same spot they were an hour ago. He usually unhitched the buggy right away. Maybe he started doing something in the barn and forgot about Tidbit. Concern poked her, then worry. Many a farmer had gotten hurt doing hard work and by the time they were found, it was too late.

The barn door squeaked as she opened it. May held her skirt close to her legs in case any daddy-long-legs spiders were lurking about, her dress swishing as she entered.

She made her way back to the milking room. "Thad?"

"I'm back here, cleaning the stanchions. Did you want something?" His voice held a note of surprise.

She found him busy, but unharmed. "You looked tired at dinner, and I wanted to make sure you were okay."

His face brightened. "*Danki* for thinking about me, but I'm fine."

"Okay, but did you know that Tidbit was still hitched?"

"Oh… I forgot about him." His voice wavered as his back straightened.

"You do have a lot on your mind these days. Ethan was on his way home and I asked him to unhitch Tidbit. I figured you forgot when I saw him still hitched after you checked the pasture."

"*Jah.* Is Elmer still up at the *haus*?"

"*Nein*, he had a tour bus coming in early in the morning so he wanted to get home."

"I'm done here, so I'll walk you back to the *haus*."

When they entered the kitchen, Josie was finishing up the dishes while Leah sat in her high chair having a treat.

May checked Leah's hands after she shoved the last bite greedily in her mouth with most of the crumbs appearing to have stuck all over her face. "What a mess."

"I'll get a washcloth," Josie said, pulling open the drawer.

May heard scuffling on the porch, then came a knock on the door.

Caleb Brenneman stuck his head through the kitchen door. "Anyone home?"

May laughed. "What are you doing, Caleb? Come in, come in."

Caleb's son Jacob strolled in first, with Sarah and Caleb following close behind him. Jacob lifted his hands until May finally noticed a midnight-black kitten wiggling in his hand.

"Oh, she is adorable. Have a seat. Would you like a cup of coffee?" She gestured to the pot on the stove.

Sarah looked at Caleb, and he shook his head. "*Nein, danki*, we just finished supper."

Caleb slapped Thad on the back. "You look as tired as I feel, my friend."

Thad nodded. "*Jah*, summer makes for long days of work. What brings you by?"

Caleb tilted his head toward his *sohn*. Jacob held the kitten out in front of him. "This is Blackie. She's a gift for Leah."

Silence filled the room as May glanced from Blackie to Thad, then back at Jacob.

"Tiger has taught her well," Jacob said. "She's a *gut* mouser."

May shot Thad a serious look. "Was this your idea? You didn't talk to me about a pet. Don't I have a say in the matter?" She tried to calm her voice. Glancing back at Thad, she noticed his flushed cheeks. She hadn't meant to voice her opinion so strongly. But this should have been a private conversation between her and Thad. "Sorry, I suppose she is old enough to treat one gently."

Caleb took a step forward. "Every farm

could use a *gut* barn cat. Keep her in the *haus* in the winter, and you won't have field mice sneaking in. I'll guarantee you."

May picked up Leah from her high chair. "Come and see your new kitty." She carried her over to Jacob.

Leah's eyes widened. She smiled and reached her hand out toward the kitten, then jerked it back. She reached out again, her hand getting closer, then finally touched the kitten with her fingertips. She giggled and jerked back.

"Is she soft and wiggly? Touch her again," May coaxed.

Jacob held out the kitten to May. She sat and held Leah and Blackie.

May looked at Thad. "*Jah*, a *kind* needs a little animal to *liebe* and play with." She raised a brow at Caleb.

Caleb put an arm around Sarah and guided her to the door. "Now that we've upset your whole night, we'll be going."

Thad walked Caleb, Sarah and Jacob out to their buggy. May pet the kitty and showed Leah how to stroke his back. The little girl smiled and watched it until her eyes grew heavy and she fell asleep.

Thad walked back in. "Sorry, I had no idea they were going to do that. I might have mentioned to Caleb that we wanted to get Leah a kitten someday, but I never thought that they had one to give away right now."

"It's okay. Leah will like playing with her, but she'll have to do it tomorrow. It's bedtime."

"For me, too. I'm tired. *Danki* for letting her keep the kitty, May." Thad kissed her cheek, then walked upstairs.

His kiss knocked the wind out of her. She dragged in a ragged breath and tried to calm her racing pulse. She hadn't expected the kiss, nor had she expected her reaction to it. After all, he was her husband. Her eyes followed him until he was out of sight.

She sighed as she got Blackie a bowl of milk and watched her lap it up. She found a box in the storage room and set the kitten in it alongside one of Leah's fuzzy stuffed kitties. The next time she checked on Blackie, she had fallen fast asleep snuggled next to her friend.

A tear welled up in May's eye until it spilled over and ran down her cheek. She brushed it away as she sat in a chair and stared at Blackie. That was the kind of unconditional love, like *Gott's* love, she wanted. She didn't want secondhand love or someone who pitied her, or someone who wanted her out of loneliness. She wanted to feel loved by someone who was content being next to her.

May wanted an adoring *ehemann* by her side, working hard as they planned their future together. She deserved that. Could she find that kind of *liebe* with Thad? Did he *liebe* her at all?

Sometimes she thought he did. Sometimes she wasn't so sure. Only *Gott* knew for certain.

Chapter Ten

Thad entered the kitchen to the unfamiliar sound of May's laughter filling the room. A cheesy aroma made his stomach growl. "Something sure smells *gut* in here so where are you three off to?" He stepped around Elmer and Josie, who was holding Leah.

Elmer lifted the picnic basket he held in one hand and nodded to the pie in his other. "Wherever these two take me, but today it's going to be to the park. Josie even made mac and cheese again."

"Do you need any help getting out to

your buggy? I could hold that pie for you, Elmer?" he teased.

Elmer laughed. "There's no chance I'm handing you this cherry pie after I've been standing here for the last ten minutes smelling it. It has my name written all over it."

May followed them out on the porch. "Are you sure you want Leah along? You don't have to take her."

"Me go, *Mamm*."

"I invited her along. We are going to have a great time with this sweet one." Josie gave Leah a little shake and Leah squealed with delight.

Thad walked over and stood next to May on the porch. They watched Elmer place the picnic basket in the back of his buggy, then help Josie and Leah into the front seat. He climbed in and settled on the seat next to them, tapped the reins on the horse's back and spurred him into a trot. They drove down the lane and onto the road, heading to the park.

Thad slipped his arm around May. "Why are they taking Leah with them on their date?"

She looked up at him and smiled. "It was Josie's idea. I think she is testing Elmer to see if he likes *kinner*, and if he is helpful with a *kind*."

"Hmm. I didn't know women set traps like that to test us poor unsuspecting men."

"I'm not saying any more on the subject. Today, I finish canning beans, so tomorrow Josie, Leah and I can attend a frolic." She tossed Thad a wry smile. "So what are you up to this afternoon?"

"I heard you say earlier that you had canning to do, and I thought I'd come and help. With twice the hands, you'll have to spend less time standing. How is your foot feeling?"

"It's been three weeks since I broke the bone and it feels *gut*. So, you ran out of work to do?"

"*Nein.* Always plenty of work on the farm. I just wanted to be helpful."

"*Datt* is *gut*. You are a man after my own heart." The look on her face told him that the words slipped out, surprising even her. She paused, then whipped out a smile that stole his heart and made this whole canning idea he'd come up with worth it.

"So what do you want me to do?"

"I already have the beans cut and the jars sterilized. So we need to start packing."

She set what they needed on the counter, set a pan of beans and clean jars in front of him, and nodded. "Go to work."

He held up his spoon. "Ready." He started scooping spoonfuls of beans and packing them into a jar. "Do you think it's getting serious between Josie and Elmer?"

"Neither one really talks about it, but they are both very happy and bubbly when they are around each other." She filled her jar and reached for a lid. He reached at the same time and his hand touched hers and lingered. The feel of her soft skin sent a streak all the way up his arm and pierced his heart. He took a deep breath, waiting for something to happen. Anything.

She didn't pull away.

"We could hurry to get the beans done and take a buggy ride into town for an ice cream cone, or just go for a ride since we don't have Leah for a little while." The words spilled out a little breathy.

She hesitated, then pulled her hand away. "I'll probably be too tired when we're done to go for a ride."

"A ride could be relaxing."

She raised a brow. "I better wait and see how I feel. I don't want to commit to that just yet."

The stop sign she held up released that streak that had hit his heart. *Jah*, he got the hint, she wasn't ready. But as the *gut* Book said, patience is a virtue. He'd wait. Little by little he was getting a little closer to her. It was only a matter of time before she'd come around.

"Hurry, Josie." May looked back as she hurried to the door. "We don't want to be late to the frolic to finish Sarah's *boppli* quilt. I'll hitch Gumdrop while you get your basket of scraps of material."

May drove the buggy to the *haus* and parked. Josie stepped into the buggy hugging Leah to her side and settled on the seat next to May.

"Giddyap, Gumdrop. No loafing, we don't want to get there when it's over."

When they turned onto the road, the horse lengthened his gait and stepped out smartly. The buggy jiggled and Leah let out a laugh as if someone were tickling her tummy.

In twenty minutes, May turned Gumdrop onto the Yoders' farm and trotted him up to the front door.

"Good mornin'," David Yoder greeted them as he took the reins. "I'll take your buggy and park it in the shade."

"*Danki*, David. We seem to be running a bit late." May grabbed Leah, Josie snatched the scrap basket and they hurried into the *haus*.

David's daughter Jane met them at the

door. "Come in. We were all wondering where you were." She waved toward the stretcher where the others sat stitching their patches on the quilt.

"*Ach*, you made it." Sarah hurried over to May and stole Leah from her arms. "Here's my sweet girl. She is getting bigger every time I see her."

Mary, Sarah's daughter, stuck her head out of the kitchen. "Is Leah here?"

"*Jah*, come see how big she is," Sarah called.

Mary scooped Leah out of Sarah's arms. "I'll take this hungry little critter back to the kitchen with me, and we'll find a cookie and lemonade."

Leah laughed at Mary as she made funny faces.

"How old is she now?" Mary asked.

"My little pumpkin has been spreading her joy for a year, but you might want to watch her. She pulls herself up now and tries to get into everything."

May sat in the empty chair next to Hannah Smith. "Hannah, it is so *gut* to see you. How are Ezra and the family?"

"Everyone is healthy, and we are looking forward to our new addition." She patted her stomach and beamed with joy.

"I see that. I'm so happy for you." May wrapped her arm around Hannah and hugged.

Christine Glick scooted over and patted Hannah's shoulder. "We will start your *boppli*'s quilt as soon as Sarah's *boppli* blanket is finished."

Janie breezed through the door as if a butterfly caught on a breeze. "*Ach*, sorry I'm late."

"Would that handsome Jonah Hochstetler be the reason why?" Christine teased. "My *ehemann* Carter said he saw you in his courting buggy."

"*Ach*, he just gave me a lift to the store." Janie batted her eyes and tilted her head with a coy smile.

"Oh!" Sarah moaned, placing her hands

around her protruding belly. "I think you better hurry with the quilt."

Christine shot to her feet. "I'll run and call the midwife! She can meet you at your *haus*, Sarah. I thought she was supposed to come to the frolic…"

"*Danki*, Christine," Sarah gasped. "Caleb is waiting outside. He brought me since it's so close to my time."

Caleb hurried in and helped Sarah out to the buggy. May couldn't help but notice his face was flushed with excitement. His and Sarah's first *boppli* was something special to both of them.

After the rush of Sarah's departure, the frolic continued until the quilt was finished. May wrestled Leah away from Mary, and Josie gathered up her scraps and basket, then they said their goodbyes and headed to their buggy to go home.

"Even though it ended a little early, I had a great time," Josie said. "But thankfully we got Sarah's *boppli* quilt finished. I have never sewed so fast in all my life." She slid onto the seat and settled next to May, situating her sewing basket on the floor of the buggy.

May handed Leah over to Josie. "She's almost asleep. The rocking of the buggy should do it."

The trip home was relaxing with the methodical clip-clop of Gumdrop's hooves tapping out a rhythm. May settled back in the seat and glanced over at Leah sleeping and Josie softly singing a hymn from the *Ausbund.*

Josie stopped singing and glanced toward May. "Do you think Janie and Jonah are courting? She said he was only taking her to the store. Do you believe that?"

May dipped her head to the side to dodge the glare of the sun. "That's two questions, but the answer is the same for both. I don't know." Amish women loved to gossip, but May wasn't going to talk about her best friend's love life.

Gumdrop turned into his home driveway without being coaxed, ready for his treat when he got back to the barn. May stopped in front of the *haus* to let Josie and Leah out. "I'll unhitch Gumdrop and be right in."

"Don't hurry, I'll put Leah down for a nap." It was nice having Josie here to help. For sure and certain, May would miss her when she went home.

May hooked the pail of oats to the stall door and headed to the *haus*, excitement bubbling in her to hear the news of Sarah's new *boppli*. She was happy for her friend. Sarah had been married to Samuel for ten years but they had never had *kinner*. After his death, she'd never planned on having the joy of a family until she married Caleb a few years ago. Now Sarah would finally be a *mamm*.

May entered the kitchen in a daze of happiness for her friend. She turned to see Thad and his mother hovering over the canned string beans on the counter. They both turned at her entrance. Thad's face was covered in regret, Gretchen's was a glare. "What's wrong?"

"What's wrong? I'll tell you what's wrong," Gretchen began. "Most of these beans you canned the other day are spoiled. The lids never sealed, and you apparently never checked them. Every woman knows to check to make sure they sealed."

May ran to the counter and gasped. Gretchen was right. The lids weren't sealed and the beans were bubbling with fermentation. She glanced up and locked eyes with Thad. "I guess I forgot."

"You forgot! Such carelessness!" Gretchen hissed.

"*Mamm*, May feels bad enough. What's done is done."

"Well, I'll leave you two to take care of the mess." Gretchen huffed to the screen door, letting it bang on her way out.

"May, I'm sorry, I must have distracted you. We started talking about other things when we were done and just forgot. I'll start taking off lids while you can get a bucket."

She hurried back and helped Thad empty the jar contents into the bucket. "I checked the first few jars when they came out of the canner. They sealed, and I guess I got busy and didn't check the others. I feel like such an idiot."

"*Nein*. I'm sure *Mamm* knows by experience, she just doesn't want to say it. Besides, it's always a lot easier to criticize someone else's work." He gave her a reassuring pat on the shoulder.

She turned toward him and he hugged her. It felt *gut* to have him stand up for her against his *mamm*, but she still felt stupid. But that wouldn't happen again.

She ached from embarrassment as she dumped a lot of hard work into the slop bucket.

Thad took a jar, opened it and dumped. "You don't have to help me," May said.

"Of course I do. We're partners. You're helping me out keeping the farm, why shouldn't I help you? We're in this together. Don't feel bad. It's the kind of error that we all make. The ones you checked should have been a *gut* indication of the whole group. It just so happened in this case they weren't."

"*Danki* for your understanding."

"How was the frolic?"

"Very exciting. In all the fuss over the beans, I forgot to tell you about it. We were all talking and having a *gut* time and all of a sudden Sarah Brenneman goes into labor. Christine called the midwife to meet Sarah at her *haus*. Fortunately, Caleb had driven Sarah over to the Yoders' and was waiting outside for her, so they could get right home."

"Wow, you don't get that kind of excitement at a frolic very often. So has she had her *boppli* yet?"

"We haven't heard yet."

It was nice just talking to Thad about her day, Sarah thought to herself. They didn't often do that. He was always so tired after working on the farm all day, and now, with her foot healing, sometimes the effort of getting around wore her out and she went to sleep early.

She glanced over at Thad. "*Danki* again for helping clean up the mess. That was so thoughtful."

When they finished the cleanup, Thad went out to do chores and May leaned a hip against the sink and stared at the counter where the beans had sat. She'd make sure that never happened again, but what hurt most was that Thad's *mamm* had scolded her like a child. Her sharp tongue cut faster than a double-edged blade.

At 7:00 p.m., a buggy came up the driveway and stopped at the *haus*. May ran to the front door. "Caleb, how is Sarah?"

"She is doing well." His smile stretched from ear to ear. "It's a boy!"

"Congratulations! Jacob will be a *gut* big *bruder* to him. Have you named him?"

"He is named after his two *grossdaedi*, Michael Paul Brenneman."

"*Datt's* a fine name. Is Mary at the bakery?"

"*Nein*. We closed the bakery for a couple of days. Mary wants to stay home with Sarah and the *boppli*. The whole family is excited."

"Of course. Tell Mary I can help when she needs it. Josie is here to watch Leah, but if Josie goes home soon, I'll just bring Leah with me."

"*Nein*, that won't be necessary. Mary has hired a friend to work in the bakery. I need to get going, I have a couple more stops to make."

"*Danki* for letting us know, Caleb." She closed the screen door and watched Caleb rush to his buggy. He waited when he saw Thad walk over from the barn. May heard the excitement in his voice as he told Thad the news.

Sadness drifted over her heart. Right now, it was doubtful she'd ever have *kinner*. After all, her and Thad's marriage was only one of convenience.

Wasn't it?

The next morning, May sat with Leah and Blackie on the grass in front of the *haus* and watched them play. Blackie hopped around jumping at bugs and birds and chasing her tail. Leah played tug-of-war with her with her chew toy. She'd hold it out, Blackie would try to get it, she'd pull it away and laugh. Leah tried to push herself to stand, but was wobbly.

"Oh, are you going to try to walk? You are so big."

Leah plopped back down, then picked up the chew toy and poked it at Blackie.

Wheels crunching over rocks and horse's hooves tromping the ground stole May's attention as Janie parked her buggy under the oak tree by the *haus*. She stepped down and ran toward May, her eyes and cheeks glazed with tears.

May jumped up and wrapped Janie in a hug. "What's wrong?"

Janie gasped for breath. "Jonah says he can't court me any longer."

"Why, did he give a reason?"

"His *mamm* told him I wasn't the right girl for him."

May could hardly believe her ears. She had no idea the extent of Gretchen Hochstetler's sway over her *buwe*. *Nein*, they weren't *buwe*, they were men. "What? He listens to his *mamm* when he wants to find a *frau*?"

"Apparently so, and you know Gretchen, she is pushy." Janie looked around. "I hope she isn't close by to hear me. That's all I need."

"*Nein*, I saw her and her *ehemann* Aaron leave the *dawdi haus* earlier and they're not back yet." May motioned at the blanket Leah was sitting on. "I'm afraid I know Gretchen only too well. Now, sit and tell me the whole story."

Her friend wiped away the tears from her cheeks and sat down. "Not much to tell really. He stopped by yesterday and said that we could no longer court, that his *mamm* said she had someone he needed to meet, and she just knew he'd *liebe* her. She wouldn't quit pestering Jonah about it until he broke it off with me." Janie sniffled, took a hanky and dried her eyes.

"He told you that?" The heat burned its way up May's neck. "So without even seeing or talking to this *mädel*, he breaks up with you?"

"Apparently so." Her shoulders shook with each sob. "I'm sorry, May."

"For what?"

"For not realizing how much it hurt you when Thad dumped you for April." Janie blew her nose. "I was really insensitive. I remember I joked around about how Thad was so cute, you should marry him. I never stopped to think how that must actually have felt."

Stunned, May straightened her back and rubbed a hand across the grass. "For Leah's sake, I pushed that behind me and haven't thought about it since Thad and I married."

"I just wanted you to know that now I understand what you went through." She patted May's arms. "I didn't mean to open old wounds and hurt you again."

"It's *oll recht*. But now that I think about it, Gretchen always did like April better than me. I wonder if she told Thad the same thing?" She swallowed hard as the thought settled upon her like the dust stirred up from galloping hooves.

If Gretchen *had* poked her nose into her and Thad's courtship, that would explain so much.

Chapter Eleven

May finished sewing her strips of rags together, then started rolling them in a ball. *Jah*, this group of blues and yellows would make a beautiful rug when she had it woven.

Thad stepped in the doorway. "So here you are." He crossed the sewing room and sat in the chair next to hers. He smelled *gut*. She tried to keep the smile off her face, but it was hard. The scent of his goat's milk soap was a little intoxicating, and he'd combed his hair. He looked so handsome.

"How's the new rug coming along?" he asked, his voice almost startling her.

"Your old shirts are going to look great alongside the yellow of this old tablecloth. What's your dairy association meeting about tonight?"

"They want to start dumping milk in protest for having to sell it at regular price. Other small farmers across the country are starting to dump."

May laid her ball of strips down and faced Thad. "What do you think?"

"I hate to dump perfectly *gut* milk, but I feel it's important to follow what the majority wants. The association members need to stick together. They'll probably take a vote tonight. But I shouldn't be home too late. They might just have a discussion, then take the vote, if not tonight, then at the next meeting. They are letting everyone think about it."

"Does discussion mean argue? Dumping sounds like a touchy subject when it comes to money. There could be strong opinions on both sides of the issue."

Thad chuckled. "*Jah*, I'm afraid you're

probably right." He glanced at the clock. "I better get going. See you later."

At 7:00 p.m., May glanced out the window. Black clouds rolled and rumbled across the evening sky. The air had turned a greenish-gray. She laid her ball of strips down and hurried downstairs to close all the windows.

When she entered the kitchen, Thad burst through the door, turned and slammed it closed.

"What's going on, Thad?"

His face was ashen. "There's a tornado coming across the field. Grab Leah and head to the basement. Where's Josie?"

May gasped. "She and Leah are both upstairs."

"New plan. I'll run up and get them. You get a lantern and go to the basement and get into the southwest corner. We'll be right down."

May scurried downstairs, hurriedly cleared the southwest corner and dragged an old mattress close so they could cover themselves with it. Within seconds, Thad was marching down the stairs holding Leah, followed by Josie close on his heels. By the time they reached her, the day had turned as black as night and the wind's howling was deafening, sounding like a freight train passing directly overhead. Thad passed Leah to May, then grabbed the mattress and held it over them.

Before the mattress covered her eyes, May glanced at the window. She could see the trees bending so far over, she feared they'd snap clean off. She heard a loud cracking, like a tree falling. Crashing sounds next to the *haus* and farther away in the distance made her squeeze Thad's arm. Glass breaking upstairs along with thumps, bumps and bangs made her huddle closer to Thad and Leah, with Josie clinging close on the other side of Thad.

Leah began to cry. May attempted to soothe her. "Shh, it'll be all right."

"*Nein*. Stop it! Stop it!" Leah screamed.

The louder the storm raged, the louder her cries grew.

"I know you're scared, but we are here to protect you," May cooed next to Leah's ear. "Shh."

Thad wrapped May and Leah in his arms. "Josie, stay close."

"*Jah*, don't worry, I will."

The wind died down and the crashing noises stopped. But the rain continued, and the hail pummeled the roof and the side of the *haus* so hard, May feared it might break the walls down. After what felt like hours, the storm finally quieted, and Thad pushed the mattress off them.

The brightening sky pulled May's attention to the basement window plastered with mud. Apparently, the pounding rain had splashed mud up from the ground. A shiver of fear ran through May's heart.

Thad started to stand but Leah clutched at his shirt. *"Nein, Daed. Nein."* He kissed Leah's head and held her close.

"Shh, the storm is over. It'll be okay. The

worst is over. It's just rain now." When she quieted, he handed her back to May and started to stand.

"Nein, Daed!" Leah screamed.

"Okay. We'll all stay here a while longer to make sure the storm has passed. Is everyone all right?"

"Jah, just scared." Josie's voice quaked.

"I'm fine." May clutched Leah close to her chest to soothe the little *mädel*. After a while, she checked Leah. "She's finally asleep," she whispered to Thad. "We need to see if we should board up windows or doors so the rain doesn't make things worse."

"I agree." Thad kissed Leah on the cheek. "Hand her to Josie and let's do a walk-through upstairs before we let them come up." He looked at Josie. "Do you mind waiting down here?"

"Nein, but could you bring us some blankets?"

"Sure, give us a minute." He grabbed May's hand as if it was the natural thing to do and helped her up the basement stairs. He paused and drew in a deep breath before he unlatched the basement door and peered out. He pushed the door open and pulled May up to the top of the stairs. She held the lantern up and moved it around in an arc as they assessed the damage.

May stared. The two west windows in the kitchen were broken and glass was scattered all over the room. The table and chairs were overturned. The cupboard doors were open and it looked like the storm had sucked everything off the shelves of one of the cabinets and thrown them around the room. They walked through the mess, Thad still clutching her hand.

The sitting room was untouched. Thad led the way upstairs. May stayed close behind, her heart pounding against her ribs at what they might find.

The empty west bedroom had a broken window and water had drenched the flooring. The rest of the second floor was untouched by the storm.

Thad looked all around. "I'll need to get the windows boarded up tonight. Let's check the outside."

"Okay, but let me run some blankets down to Josie first."

Thad was waiting in the kitchen for her when she came up from the basement.

"Ready?" He flashed an encouraging smile. She nodded and he threw open the door.

He stepped onto the porch first, and she followed. It was 7:40 p.m. The sun breaking through the clouds was just setting, giving her enough light to see around the farm as they stepped off the porch.

May swept her gaze from one side of the barnyard to the other. The barn and shed roofs lay scattered over the barnyard and field. Several trees were down and debris strewn all around. She pressed a hand to her chest. "It's going to cost a lot of money to repair these buildings."

Thad nodded. "Money we don't have for something as massive as this damage. I'm going to walk out into the pasture. Do you want to come along?"

"*Jah.* We do this together." She glanced his way, trying to focus through tear-filled eyes. He wrapped his arm around her shoulders and held her close to him as they walked out to the pasture. She scanned the land and saw that several cows were dead.

Thad murmured, "I count twelve down."

May's throat tightened as she burst into tears. "What are we going to do? There is so much damage."

"I'm not sure. I don't have the money to repair all this. We can borrow from an Amish lender but the farm is barely making ends meet right now. I'm not sure where the extra money for the loan repayment will come from. Look at that field." He pointed to the fall crop of squash and pumpkins. "It looks like a total loss but I'm hoping in the morning I can salvage some. I've been counting on the fall market. In order to survive, we'll need a bumper crop next year and for milk prices to go up."

May surveyed the *haus* as they walked back. It didn't look bad, but a lot of shingles were missing, which meant the *haus* roof would have to be reshingled. Thad let go of her hand and turned all around examining the land again. His shoulders slumped.

Raindrops hit May's hand, then quickly turned to a light shower. She ran up the porch steps while Thad kept looking around.

"So much destruction, but it could have been worse. If every Amish farmer around here has this much damage, there won't be enough money in our community to pay for all the damages. Everyone chips in, but that won't work for this much damage." When it started to rain harder, he jumped up the porch steps two at a time and plopped down in a chair next to May.

He glanced her way. "I don't know how we will ever recover from this."

She reached over and patted his arm. "The bishop will put the word out to the other Amish communities asking for help.

We don't know, maybe it's just our farm that got this much damage."

"You're right, and it could have been a lot worse." He gave her an encouraging smile. "I'm going to check the milk room and get a hammer and some plywood to cover the broken windows until we can get them fixed. You better let Josie know she can come up but Leah needs to stay off the floor until we sweep."

"If she's still asleep, I'll just put her to bed and start cleaning up."

Thad gave her a hug. "We'll get through this." The feeling of his arms was comforting on so many different levels. He kissed her forehead and took his arms away. The cool air that passed between them when he stepped away let her know what she was missing.

She smiled up at him. "*Jah,* we will. Together."

Thad's gut wrenched as he gazed out over his farm. *Nein.* His and May's farm, and it was barely breaking even now. This would be devastating, but he couldn't let May know just how bad it really was for them. If he lost her family's farm, she'd never forgive him. It had been one of the stipulations in their marriage bargain. *Jah,* they were getting along better, but was their relationship *gut* enough to withstand a catastrophe like this? The farm meant everything to May. He swallowed against the glumness.

He opened the barn door and made his way to the milking room. Doing a careful walk-through, he surveyed the whole area. Aside from the roof being gone, he didn't observe any other damage inside of the barn. First thing tomorrow, he'd see if he could get a tarp put over the rafters until he could make arrangements to replace the roof. The barn had numerous floor drains, but nonetheless, he had to stop the rain and other elements from entering and doing any further damage.

When the rain finally let up, he dashed

over to the shed and cut several pieces of plywood for the *haus* windows. He carried them to the *haus* and May helped him nail the pieces in place.

When that was finished, he and May helped Josie sweep all the glass off the floor and clean up the mess in the kitchen.

Thad glanced at the clock. Midnight. "Let's go to bed. We'll need our rest for tomorrow."

The next morning, Thad quickly ate his breakfast. He kept glancing outside as dawn began to light the barnyard.

"More pancakes, Thad?" May asked.

"*Nein*, I need to get out and assess the damage in the daylight to determine how much to request on a loan. Looking down the road, there is a lot of damage to neighboring farms. I need to get our application in before the Amish lender runs out of money."

"Josie, will you watch Leah while I go out and help Thad?"

"Of course, May. I'm here...to help."

Thad grabbed a tablet and pencil. They stepped into their boots by the door and walked out into the field.

He opened the tablet and handed it to May. "Your handwriting is better. I'll let you write it down." He walked down a field row and May followed. "Last night, I'd hoped that we could save a few pumpkins and squash but this is a total loss for sure. The storm uprooted the vines and smashed the pumpkins and squash back on the ground. Some even looked like they had exploded."

Next he checked each field, all the livestock, and did a thorough assessment of the buildings.

Thad gazed out over the barnyard. "I'll have the *youngies* clean all this up. Let's go check the barn." He glanced over at May. Her face told him how hurt she was to see all the damage. "We'll get it fixed, May, don't worry." He wrapped an arm around her, and she leaned into him for support.

"Last night you sounded like the loan repayment would probably stretch us beyond what we could afford," she said.

"We'll talk to the lender and see what we can work out. Don't worry just yet." But her face told him she didn't believe that.

He opened the barn door, and she went in first. The stanchions and stalls all looked intact. The flooring and walls of the barn were unharmed. Thad told her what needed marked down that he thought needed repair. He wanted to make sure to request a loan that would cover all the repair costs.

After their evaluation of the farm, he went to his desk and tallied up the damages. His estimate ran in the thousands of dollars. Money he didn't have and wouldn't for a long time. He had to decide if he wanted to go with the traditional shingle roof on the barn or change to a steel roof. If he wanted to go cheaper, he could go to aluminum. But the *haus* definitely needed shingling, too. The roofs alone would probably run over $100,000.

He stood up and paced the floor behind

his desk, running his hands through his hair. He finally looked up and saw May standing in his office doorway.

"Thad, how does it look?"

He swiped his hand down his beard. "I'm worried about borrowing all this money and getting it repaid, but there's no choice."

May took a step forward. "I know, but I have an idea on how to get the money and pay off the debt."

"My first priority is to get the loan papers filled out and sent in. You can tell me about your rug business or whatever after that. The loan is the best way to get this much money." He patted her arm and smiled.

Chapter Twelve

May's gaze swept over Thad's face. The second day after the storm, and he looked tired after a stressful day of filling out forms to borrow money.

"Now that the loan papers have been sent, would it be possible to get a cup of coffee while I listen to your plan to get money or make money? I have a feeling this might be a long talk."

"Of course. Let's go sit at the kitchen table." She poured two cups, set them on the table and sat in the chair next to his. "Before you left for the last dairy association meeting, you said they wanted to start dumping milk and they were going to take a vote. In all the commotion since the storm, I forgot to ask, did the vote pass?"

"Yes. They want to start dumping milk."

May pressed her back against the chair. "We can't afford to waste milk like that. So I've been thinking…"

"What about?" His voice sounded tired.

She laid her hand on his arm, then quickly pulled it away. Her cheeks burned at her familiar gesture. She gulped a breath. "Elmer showed Josie and me all around his cheese factory. He said they ship all over the world and that his business was doing *gut*."

"So why are you telling me this?"

"I think we should make cheese instead of pouring the milk on the ground. We could even make ice cream."

Thad leaned back in his chair. "I don't have the time or the money to make cheese in addition to farming. And it would cost a fortune to set it up. Not to mention, I don't know a thing about cheese. Elmer sells a lot, but he makes all kinds of fancy artisan cheese and sells it to the tourists, the *Englisch*."

"But listen…"

He held up a hand. "*Honig*, I don't have the money to start up a cheese factory, and especially now after the storm."

"But I do."

He straightened his back. "Where did you get that kind of money?"

"I've worked all my life selling rugs, quilts, doilies and baked goods. I've operated a vegetable stand and saved all my money. I have always lived here, and *Daed* or you have always supported me. I have over $100,000 saved."

Thad gasped. "I can't believe it. But even if you have the money, we don't know a thing about making cheese or starting a factory."

May laid a hand over his hand. "We can learn. Let's at least check into it."

She noticed his gaze drop to her hand on his. His voice shook. "I don't have time to learn how to start a cheese factory and then run it, while keeping the farm going."

"Why don't we hire more *youngies*? And I'll help, too. Maybe I'll run the cheese factory."

"You know what the bishop thinks about women working outside the home." He gave her a serious look.

"*Jah*, but we have to make money soon or we'll lose the farm. Our fall crop is gone, we have lost almost half our herd of cows and we have to borrow money with interest. We have to have some way to get back on our feet. It doesn't have to be a big factory like Elmer's. I can make cheese and sell it at my vegetable stand. I will have to start small anyway while I'm learning."

He leaned over and gave her a sweet kiss on the lips. "May, you are one gutsy lady."

Heat rose from her neck onto her cheeks and burned her ears. Her voice nearly stuck in her throat. "I'll take that compliment as a yes."

"What is a yes?" Gretchen asked as she

opened the screen door and entered, followed by Aaron, Thad's *daed*.

May tried to stare Thad into silence.

"*Mamm*, we are thinking of starting a cheese factory." Thad's words seemed to suggest he was aiming to shock more than inform. "Elmer is very successful at his cheese business."

"Indeed he is. He is a cheese artisan. You are not. You are a farmer."

"He farms, too."

"He doesn't farm the land. He only has his milk cows," Gretchen huffed. "You'd have to build the factory from scratch."

"We know that."

"I wouldn't be surprised if this was May's idea."

"It is *our* idea to try to save the farm. We can't keep selling cheap milk or dumping it on the ground because we have no buyers. Cheese can be packaged and sold all over the world."

"You'll lose the shirt off your back if you waste your money on starting a factory.

And who will do all that work?" Gretchen jabbed her fists on her hips. "It's a crazy idea. You are foolish to sink your money into such a business."

Aaron pulled his *frau* toward the door. "Gretchen, it is their business, not ours."

"Thad is not sinking a dime into this business. I am." May let the truth slip out, then was angry with herself for letting Gretchen provoke her into saying it. "The money is mine, and don't forget this farm has been in my family for 170 years. Thad inherited it from my sister. The farm isn't making enough right now to pay all the bills and support us."

"Apparently it does if you have enough money saved to sink into a cheese business," Gretchen hissed.

Thad placed a firm hand on May's shoulder. "*Nein. Mamm, danki* for the advice, and we will take it under consideration."

Aaron pushed Gretchen out the door, then turned back. "I'm sorry about that, *sohn.*"

Thad patted May's arm. "*Mamm* is not

an adventurer when it comes to money. She still has a coffee can on her kitchen counter filled with money saved up for a winter coat for me when I was a *bu*."

May raised a brow. "So you didn't get a new coat?"

"She decided to save the money and sewed those little knit cuffs on the end of the sleeves of my old coat. I was growing up, not out, so it still fit just a little short. The cuffs did the trick, and she's been patting herself on the back for her thriftiness ever since."

"When winter comes, I'm going to check the sleeves on your coat and see if you need a new one."

He laughed. "*Jah*, I believe you will. Don't let *Mamm* get you down. She grew up in a family where they didn't have much money, and every penny was saved and not spent frivolously."

May stood. "So you think I'm frivolous?" His words were like a punch on the arm. "If I have $100,000 saved, that doesn't sound frivolous to me."

"*Nein*, I didn't say that."

"It sure sounded like that to me. Are you taking her side? Do you think the cheese factory is a bad idea?" She punched her fists on her waist.

Thad stood. "Look, I know nothing about making cheese, or how to run a business like that. Yes, I see people doing it. Cheese is big business in Iowa. It might work. I just don't know." He let his gaze drop to the floor, then looked back at May. "I just don't want you to lose all your hard-earned money." Worry lined his eyes.

"So you think this is a boondoggle idea?" Her voice softened.

"Don't put words in my mouth and start a fight I don't want to have. We have been getting along so *gut, jah*?"

May walked to the sink, took a rag and wiped up around the edge. "So you just want me to put my money back in the coffee can?"

"I'm saying it's a lot of money, so we need to be certain what we want to do with it. Yes, let's inquire about starting a cheese business. Maybe we can begin small. We can always start with a couple of different cheeses and you can try selling it on your vegetable stand."

"We can start out small to learn but a small business that makes a few dollars doesn't pay very many big bills. We have to invest in our future and in our children's future." What did she just say—their children? "We will have to ensure we have enough money to make the loan payments."

Thad walked to the sink and stood next to her. "We haven't even discussed what kind of cheeses we want to make. Do you know what kinds sell the best? Didn't Elmer start out small, then add his fancy cheese the *Englisch* like?"

"*Jah*, you're right," May said. "Let's think about it and decide if it is truly right for us. In the meantime, I'll just keep making quilts and rugs and selling my vegetables."

He put an arm around her shoulders and hugged. Then his arms encircled her and pulled her close. He dropped his mouth to hers for a tender kiss.

She stepped back and exhaled. "I know what you're doing, Thad. And I don't like it. You're trying to change the subject, and you're hoping this all goes away."

"May, I have to run the farm and oversee the repairs. I don't have time to run a cheese factory, too. I'm sorry."

"I know, but the money is mine. I'll take care of running the cheese factory."

Thad's face turned somber. "The bishop won't like you running a factory, but he probably won't be against you selling a few homemade cheeses." He headed toward the other room, but looked back at May. "I'll help as much as I can. See if you can find some classes we can take, but not from Elmer." He raised a brow. "Maybe there is a book we can buy or some recipes."

She ran over and gave him a hug and a kiss on the cheek. "*Danki*, Thad. I know we can do this."

He raised a brow. "Hope so."

A burst of excitement flooded her heart. *Jah*, she could do this and the cheese factory would be a success. And she knew the perfect place to start.

The next morning, while Josie watched Leah, May hired a driver and had him drop her off at the library in Iowa City. Thad stayed at the farm to oversee the first day of repairs, but May needed to start the factory research before her boot came off and Josie went back home. She asked the librarian to show her how to find the online cheese-making class. The computer was an awkward device, but with the help of the librarian, she managed. It was a long day of studying and note taking.

On her second visit to the library, Thad went along with May. They took the advanced online cheese-making class to learn how to make the artisan cheese, then ordered a suggested recipe book and information on how to start a cheese-making business.

The following day, Thad accompanied her to visit a factory. The tour guide was helpful and answered their questions. On the way home, she asked the driver to stop at a shop so they could pick up a vat, press and other supplies. After selecting a few items, May looked up to see Thad frowning. "Is there something wrong?"

"The vat and warmer are pricey. But I guess we have to have a little outlay first. I just worry about the bills."

"*Jah*, and I forgot to tell you, we need to buy a goat or two so I can make some goat-milk cheese."

He frowned.

She knew the factory was a big risk for their family but they had to take it. They'd start out small and only increase production if it looked like the customers liked their product. With the over-production of organic milk by the big producers, it made sense to have another outlet for their milk instead of dumping it. *Jah*, she was sure she could make the cheese and sell it.

Maybe she'd offer a cheese-tasting when she officially opened her business. In the fall, she would add apples and pears to the stand from their trees. It would be easy to add cheese to the wares offered.

This had to work. Gott, *please bless the cheese idea so it will work and save the farm.*

May made her first batch of cheese and tasted it. Terrible. She threw away her second attempt. Cheese-making was a little more complicated than she'd thought. She hadn't realized that it was the aging process that actually gave cheese its distinctive taste and texture, which produced thousands of varieties. That aging caused sour, sharp or tangy tastes over time, so some of the cheeses would take several months to age properly for the taste to develop. She hadn't planned on that.

May selected a few cheeses to start with: Colby, cheddar, provolone, Monterey Jack and Parmesan. Fortunately, all cheese started with the same basic ingredients: milk, from either a cow, goat, sheep or buffalo; bacterial culture; rennet and salt.

While some of the cheese aged, she still needed something to sell. Leafing through her recipe book, she found cream cheese, sour cream, ricotta and feta cheese recipes.

For two weeks, May worked hard making cheese, throwing away batch after batch. Her stomach ached from worry that they'd lose the farm. *Nein*. She had to keep trying.

Finally, the batches started to develop good flavors. This might actually work!

A horn honked from the driveway, and May ran to look out the window. "Josie, the driver is here to take me to the doctor's office. Hopefully it won't take long."

"I'm going to pack so I'll be ready to go home when you get back."

May slid into the car and handed the driver the address. "It's a medical building."

"Yep, I've been there before, ma'am. Have you there in no time. I'm James, by the way. I'll drop you off and wait for you in the lobby."

"Thank you. That will be *gut*." Her hands fidgeted on her lap. After six weeks, she was so ready to get this boot off.

She blew out a sigh as she exited the car and hurried to the doctor's office, leaving James to follow behind her. She signed in, took a seat and waited.

"May Hochstetler," a lady in blue scrubs called.

The nurse took her information, then led her to a room to wait for the doctor. In only a minute or two, she heard paper rustling outside the door, then the doctor entered.

Dr. Kincaid held out his hand and shook

hers. "Good morning, May. Good to see you. How's the foot feeling?"

"*Gut*, Doctor. I'm anxious to get this boot off."

He loosened the bootstraps and helped her slip her foot out. He felt around her ankle and foot. He moved the foot this way and that and rubbed his hand across the top. "The foot feels like it's healed. You don't need to wear the boot in the house, but if you walk on the ground where it's uneven, wear the boot outside for another month. That'll ensure the foot doesn't twist and get reinjured."

"Do I need to come back?" She held her breath.

"Not unless you have trouble with it."

"Then I can stand on it and run my cheese business?"

He nodded. "You sure can but let your foot tell you if it gets tired. If it does, let it rest. Don't push it. It might still be weak for another few weeks."

She hopped off the examining table.

"Danki." May shivered as excitement streaked through her. Now she could officially start her business. Her plans for her factory were already down on paper. She was ready to go.

Her happy energy propelled her out of the car when it stopped in front of the *haus*. She paid the driver and hurried inside.

Josie met her at the door, her suitcase packed and sitting in the kitchen. She flagged May's driver and he agreed to give her a ride home.

"I'm going to miss you so much, Josie. And so will Leah."

Josie gave her a big hug. "I know, but I have to get home and help *Mamm*. Leah is in her high chair having lunch. Oh, and she is toddling around today."

"Tell *Aent* Matilda I said *hullo*, and that I appreciate her lending you to us for a few weeks. I hope your stay here wasn't too boring, but meeting a handsome cheesemaker may have eased the boredom just a bit, I think." Her cousin raised a brow, then hurried down the porch steps toward the waiting driver.

May stuck her head in the *haus* to check on Leah, then stepped back out on the porch to watch Josie drive away.

A feeling of loneliness settled in her chest. Waving at Josie only made it worse. She was going to miss her terribly.

Now May and Thad were truly alone as a married couple. Was she ready for a real relationship with him?

Chapter Thirteen

May gazed out the kitchen window and smiled. Without fail, every morning Thad always brought her fresh, foamy milk to use in her cheese business.

As he passed by the *dawdi haus*, Gretchen dashed out the door and appeared to be talking to him. Gretchen was always interfering. What did his *mamm* want this time? Her cucumbers picked or her carrots and potatoes dug?

May regretted her unkind thoughts. But why did that woman have to be so narrow-minded? Gretchen was always belittling her to Thad and keeping him busy so he couldn't help her with the cheese business.

Thad smiled as he finished talking to Gretchen and continued on to the *haus*. His *mamm* disappeared back into the *dawdi haus*. Letting the screen door bang behind her. That was odd, since Gretchen never banged a screen door. Ever.

"Here's your morning milk, May," Thad said upon entering the kitchen.

"*Danki* for bringing it up to the *haus*. How are repairs going on the barn?"

"They will soon be done. These men from Shipshewana really know their business." He headed for the door. "How is your foot feeling today?"

"*Jah*, it feels *gut* without the brace and I'm glad. My foot is so much cooler without all that plastic wrapped around it."

"I think it's called thermoplastic. Where is Leah?"

"Making cheese." Leah pushed herself up from sitting on the floor on the other side of the table. She held up the ball of cheese she was trying to push into a mold.

"Oh, you are a big helper, aren't you?" he praised her, then winked at May. "I can see you have a big helper."

"The best helper. I told her she could make you some cheese." She gave him a wry smile.

"I'm sure I'll like it very much." He tossed May a grin before disappearing out the door.

A knock sounded on the door before she could even count to ten. Thad must have forgotten to tell her something. At the continued silence, she looked up. "*Ach*, Janie, come in. I'm so glad to see you."

Janie gave her a hug, then sat at the kitchen table. "How's the cheese business going? *Mamm* is finished with her canning, so I thought I'd come over to see if I can help you. It's all over town about your cheese business. I think Elmer is even a little worried about his Sunnyhill business falling off with you making cheese so close to him."

"Did he say something?"

"*Nein*, I don't think so. He is just used to getting all the business around here. You will be his competition, don't forget."

"The dairy farmers around here are all dumping milk. Once I get the business going, I'm hoping to be able to buy more milk."

Janie shook her head. "Why doesn't Thad just buy more cows and supply the milk for you?"

"Maybe, we'll see. But I might need a bigger *haus*. I converted the pantry to storage for the cheese business. Thad made floor-to-ceiling shelves in there to accommodate the cheese that needed to age. And I've realized that I need an assistant. Would you be interested in the job?"

"*Jah*, I'll help. I have plenty of free time."

"Are you and Jonah still not back together?"

"*Nein*, that's over. Whatever Gretchen said to him, she killed our relationship."

May walked over and gave Janie a hug. "I'm so sorry to hear that. When do you want to start helping?"

"Now is *gut* for me. I heard Josie went home, so I thought I'd help you if you needed it." Janie's face was somber, then brightened. "Who knows, maybe I will meet some tall, handsome man by working for you."

May shot her friend a sympathetic look. "If Jonah has to have his *mamm* pick a *frau* for him, you don't want him."

"*Jah*, I know. Just tell my heart that, it's breaking in two."

"We are going to be so busy making cheese, you won't even have time to think about him."

"I hope that is true, and that your business makes lots of money," Janie laughed.

"Saturday, I'm going to have my vegetable and fruit stand. I'm going to make a few apple pies and strudels, and have a cheese-tasting here on the wraparound porch. So you can help with that."

"Do you have cheese ready to sell?"

"I have some, but I was hoping to take some advance orders. Most of our clients will probably be *Englisch*. Mr. Kolb from the gift shop in town where I consign some doilies and rugs has a computer and made me a few signs and flyers to hand out. He also said I could leave some samples with him on Friday and Saturday, and maybe some coupons to encourage the *Englisch* to drive out here." She finished the goat-cheese cheesecakes and set them aside. "We will sell these on Saturday."

"You're definitely going to give Elmer some competition. He's not going to like that."

"Elmer is on the Iowa Cheese Roundup and in the Iowa Cheese Club. He has plenty of customers."

"I don't know. He's very protective of his business."

"He has tour buses that stop at his factory. I'm sure he's not worried about a little competition. Besides, it's more than likely that *he* will drive *me* out of business, not the other way around."

"Who is Elmer driving out of business?" Thad entered the kitchen silently, almost as if he were in stocking feet.

"How long have you been out there listening to us?" May asked.

"I just came in. You two were so busy worrying about Elmer that you didn't hear me. It might serve Elmer right to have a little competition. He acts so smug, with all the tour buses stopping by his factory." Thad took off his hat and tossed it on the peg by the door. "What's for supper?"

"Baked chicken smothered in cheese. Janie has come to work for me and help out with the cheese business."

"*Gut.* Now I won't have to dump milk." Leah toddled over to her *daed*, and he picked her up and set her on his knee. "Are you going to be a cheesemaker, too?" She shook her head and smiled.

"Repairs are done," he told May. "The *youngies* are going to milk the cows the rest of the week, and I am going to help you make cheese so you will have plenty ready to sell on Friday and Saturday." He flashed her a smile.

"Really? Or are you just teasing me?"

"*Nein*, no teasing. I'm going to help, for sure and certain. Whatever you need me to do. At your tasting, I have two *youngies* that are going to stand by the road at your vegetable stand and their sister will be on the porch selling the cheese and taking orders."

Her eyes locked with his, and sent her heart racing.

Leah jumped off Thad's knee and toddled to May, holding out her arms. "*Mamm, Mamm.*"

"You want a taste of cheese?"

Leah smiled and nodded.

May gave her a small taste of the feta cheese. Leah smacked her lips and chewed, then made a funny expression. She took a piece out of her mouth and handed it back to May.

"*Danki*, sweetheart, but you are a bad advertisement for my cheese," May laughed.

The rest of the week, they all worked making feta and ricotta cheese, cream cheese and mascarpone. Some of the Gouda had aged and she had mozzarella sticks. She added flavoring, tomato bits and avocados and then made cheese spreads for crackers. She made cheese dips out of the sour cream to serve with chips, and she made mascarpone and used it for a cannoli filling.

Janie prepared many of the foods to complement the cheeses and when Saturday arrived, Thad assisted her in setting up the porch with display areas. As customers started dropping by, he helped take orders. The prepackaged feta, ricotta, cream cheese and mascarpone were big sellers.

May watched Thad's brother Jonah approach the house and take a plate of food. He glanced toward Janie but didn't approach her.

May could see the blush on Janie's cheeks rising to a cherry red, and tears begin to form in her eyes. She brushed them away when she thought no one looked.

"I'll get more samples," Janie said, and disappeared inside the *haus*.

May's sister Sadie parked her buggy under the oak tree and brought her three children up the porch steps.

May gave her sister a hug. "*Danki* for stopping by." She gave the *kinner* a piece of pizza and a glass of lemonade and had them sit in chairs by a table. They were very happy with that. They didn't get pizza that often, she imagined.

"May, I can't believe you made all these cheeses by yourself. Who would have guessed you had a talent for this?" Sadie filled her plate with several samples and sat by the *kinner*. "These are all so *gut*."

"Hope you spread the word to your friends and neighbors, *jah*?"

"*Mamm* would have been so proud of

you. I haven't seen Gretchen yet. What does she think about all this?"

May sighed. "Don't really think she approves."

"She will when she sees what a big success it is. Making all these dishes and letting everyone sample the flavors of the cheese was a great idea. Has Elmer been here yet?"

"*Nein*, not yet."

Sadie smiled at her sister. "I always thought Elmer was sweet on you. I wonder what he's going to think now that you are going to be in competition with him."

"There is plenty of business for all of us, and besides, Elmer is well established in his cheese factory. I'm sure he doesn't have to worry about our little business."

"I need to get going, or my *kinner* will eat you out of all your sample pizza. See you on Sunday."

Just as Sadie drove her buggy out onto the road, Elmer steered his into the driveway. May watched him park. She wondered if he would stop by and sample her cheese. She watched as he walked up to the porch.

"So you are starting a cheese business?" He took a piece of pizza and nibbled on it. "*Gut* cheese and pizza. What gave you the idea?"

She wasn't going to confess that they needed the money. It was none of his business. "We didn't like the idea of dumping milk, and this was a good way to use it."

He nodded. "You are right, this is a better idea. I wish you success in your new endeavor."

"*Danki*, Elmer. That means a lot coming from you. And I hope you don't feel that we are stepping on your toes."

"*Nein*, there is enough business for all of us. But you will give me some stiff competition if you keep serving food with your cheese products on them." He took a piece of the Gouda and popped it into his mouth. "*Gut* tangy flavor. All the best, May." He gave a nod to Thad as he headed back toward his buggy.

Thad worked his way through the crowd of customers on the porch over to May. "What did Elmer say?"

"He said the cheese had *gut* flavor."

"That is high praise coming from him." He watched as Elmer's buggy headed down the road. "Think he is worried just a little bit?"

May chuckled. "*Nein*. He's not worried about me making a few dollars. But he did grow quiet when he tasted a couple of my cheeses. I'm so pleased at the turnout today, and I think we have made a few regular customers."

Thad patted her shoulder. "Your cheese is *gut*, and I'm sure you will have a lot of repeat customers." He sounded impressed and that sent warmth straight to May's heart.

Could they really do this? Would this cheese-making business really help them save the farm?

May knew only *Gott* had the answers to such questions. But it didn't hurt to ask Him for guidance.

Chapter Fourteen

On Monday morning, May had set to work early starting new batches of cheese when she heard the wheels of a buggy crunch over the rock in the driveway. She glanced at the clock. Janie was early. Which was *gut*, since there was lots to do that day.

A knock sounded on the door "Come in, Janie. Don't be shy." She stayed at the sink washing some bowls.

"*Gut* mornin', May." Bishop Yoder's voice startled her.

"Bishop, I'm sorry, I thought you were Janie. Come in. Would you like a cup of coffee?"

"That would be nice." He pulled out a

chair at the kitchen table, and by the time he sat down, the cup was in front of him.

"Are you looking for Thad? I think he is in the barn."

"*Nein.* I've come to see you." He blew on his hot coffee, then took a generous sip. "I heard you made quite a stir over the weekend, giving away samples of your cheese from your new business."

May glanced at the bishop, not liking where this conversation was headed. "Many enjoyed the samples. Would you like to try any cheese?"

"*Nein.*" He shook his head as if to reinforce his reply. "May, it is Satan whispering in your ear that makes you think that a job outside the home is more rewarding than homemaking. You must not be fooled by his lies."

May stopped what she was doing, rinsed her hands and faced the bishop. "Bishop, we are losing money every day on the farm. The dairy association wants us to dump milk on the ground. We cannot afford that. We lost our fall crop in the tornado, and if that wasn't enough, we had so much damage that Thad had to take out a loan. A loan that we cannot repay without a bumper crop next year, which we cannot plan on."

"A *gut frau* has many talents to utilize in order to make money. In fact, I hear you have several thousands of dollars stashed away from your numerous projects."

"That money is still not enough to pay for the tornado damage, not to mention the loss of money in crops, and the continued dumping of milk. We won't even have money to buy seed next year at this rate."

"That is not an excuse for you to work outside of the home."

"I am not working outside the home. I am here in this *haus* every day, cooking my *ehemann*'s dinner."

"You are starting a cheese business as witnessed by everyone in the community."

"It is up to my *ehemann* and me what kind of business we own, Bishop. We do not need the community's approval to keep body and soul alive. I am not doing it for pride but to save my family's 170-year-old farm. We Amish all dress alike so no one will look wealthier than another, but we all know some have more money than others."

"May?"

Thad was standing in the kitchen doorway, his face red. His eyes shot a warning to her. "We do not talk to the bishop like that." His voice trembled.

May dropped her gaze. "You are right." She leveled her gaze at the bishop. "I'm sorry, Bishop Yoder."

The bishop stood up and slowly walked to the door, shaking his head. He turned back. "Thad, make sure it is for the right reason you start this business." He walked out the front door.

Silence fell over the kitchen.

When May heard the buggy wheels heading down the driveway, she turned toward Thad. "Your *mamm* told him."

"There was no need. Everyone in the

community knows about the cheese business," he retorted.

"He knew I had saved money, so your folks—or better yet, your *mamm*—must have told him."

"We don't know that."

"No one else knew except your parents." Thad's gaze dropped to the floor.

"Unless…did you tell others, Thad?"

"I…may have."

"I cannot believe you did that!" May turned her back on him and got busy at the sink. "You had no right to do that. And you didn't stick up for me. You never do. When your *mamm* is browbeating me, you never say a word."

"She is my *mamm*, I can't sass her."

"And I am your *frau*. I am doing all this work to save the farm. Our farm. It is what we discussed. It's what we decided to do. I'm not losing this farm. I thought we agreed on that?"

"May, you know what the *Ordnung* says as well as I do. Women take care of the home, and they should find satisfaction in that."

She stared at him. "And men are to make the living. I shouldn't have to help with that. Whether the bishop likes it or not, I'm not stopping the cheese-making until we can save the farm."

"Then you plan to stop?"

"It's a lot of work, and I don't enjoy standing on my feet making all that cheese, in addition to the cooking and taking care of the *haus*. But I will do it as long as we need to earn extra money to save the farm. Who knows, maybe I'll have enough customers that I can sell my recipes and the business."

Thad smiled. "I said it before, and I'll say it again. You're one gutsy lady." He walked over and gave May a hug. "I'll talk to Bishop Yoder and smooth things over with him. Tell him you working like this is only temporary."

"*Danki*, Thad. We have to do what we have to do."

Footsteps climbing the porch echoed into the room. Only they were lighter of foot than a man's and May knew whom they belonged to, but a second heavier set followed. She was glad of that.

The screen door squeaked open. "*Hullo*, Gretchen, *hullo*, Aaron."

"Well, I see the bishop paid you a visit. No secret what he was probably doing here. Did he tell you that you needed to stop this nonsense of running a cheese business?" Gretchen spit out the last few words.

May bit her tongue. She'd had enough of discussing her business with people that shouldn't be sticking their noses where they didn't belong. Just then she heard Leah wake from her nap.

She headed for the stairs. "Excuse me."

After May left the kitchen, Thad turned to his mother. "*Mamm*, May is a hard worker and she is only doing what she thinks is right to hold on to this land. Why do you keep needling her?"

"She is nothing like April."

Thad rubbed the back of his hand across his mouth. "April was *gut* and kind, considerate and a hard worker. May is all those things, too. We are married now. I wish you would try to get along with her. Were you the one that sent the bishop over here?"

"Everyone in the community knows she is starting a business. That is not a secret."

"Here is one thing that you and the rest of the community might not know. May has my blessing to run the cheese business, and I plan to spend as much time as I possibly can with her to make it a success. The cheese she makes is actually delicious. Did you try any of it?"

His *daed* shook his head. "*Nein*, I was too busy in my woodworking shop to try samples of cheese."

"Like I said, they were *gut*. Even Elmer said they were *gut*. And by the look on his face, he actually seemed a little concerned that she might just steal business from the Sunnyhill Cheese Factory."

Gretchen harrumphed. "That'll be the day."

"You should try the cheese, *Mamm*, before you make a statement like that. I'm telling you, it is really *gut*."

Thad watched Janie pull her buggy up to the *haus*. "I'll walk you two out. The girls have a lot of work to do, and I know May does not want to stand around arguing with you about whether she should have the cheese business or not."

Thad paused on his way down the porch steps. "May is upstairs with Leah. Give a call and let her know you have arrived."

May was already downstairs waiting in the kitchen when Janie stepped through the door. She peeked out the window to make sure Gretchen was headed back to the *dawdi haus*.

"Something wrong?" Janie asked. "You are all acting strange."

"The bishop paid me a visit this morning. He lectured me on what the *Ordnung* expects of a woman. That she is to find satisfaction working in the home only, not running a business. I think Gretchen put him up to it."

"That doesn't sound like Bishop Yoder. I've never known him to listen to anything a woman said." Janie tried to hold a straight face, then burst into laughter.

May laughed. "I'm fine, But how are you? Did Jonah talk to you at all on Saturday?"

Janie walked over to the high chair. Leah held out the piece of bread she was eating to her. "Hmm, is that *gut*?"

Leah nodded, took another bite, then offered it again to Janie.

"Oh, *danki*, but you can eat it." She walked back toward May. "It hurt to see him. I thought I could keep my feelings under control, but it was difficult to do. Have you heard if he is courting someone?"

"I haven't heard. I can ask Thad if you want me to and see if he knows."

"*Nein*, please don't do that. I don't want

him to know that I was asking about him. Not that it really matters. I just don't want to give him the satisfaction that I still care about him. I would be mortified if he found out."

"Don't worry, I won't say a thing, but I'll keep my eyes and ears open."

"I was just curious as to whom Gretchen set him up with." Janie's voice dipped.

"I can't believe how her sons think the sun rises and sets on her opinion. Thad is the same way. We had words this morning because he didn't stick up for me. I'm certain Gretchen was the one that sent the bishop to my door."

"Maybe if we ever have sons, they will think that about us." Janie took a deep breath and stood up straight. "Are you ready to start making the cheese? I need to keep my hands and mind busy."

"We are going to make the same cheese recipes again for this weekend, and I have a few special orders that we need to get started on."

"Before we do anything, I have a little gossip to tell you." Janie had a twinkle in her eye and seemed, at least temporarily, back to her old self.

"And what is that?"

"Guess who I saw in Elmer's courting buggy the other day?"

May's heart nearly stopped. If it was anyone but Josie, she'd never be able to tell her. She'd seen the hurt in Janie's eyes and didn't want to see it in Josie's eyes, too. Why was it that all three of them seemed to be unhappy in *liebe*?

"Who was it?" She nearly choked the words out.

"Josie."

May felt overwhelming relief. "Really? I'm so happy for her." At least there was one Amish man in their community who was loyal.

Chapter Fifteen

On Church Sunday, May relaxed on the buggy seat next to Thad as he steered Tidbit past the white picket fence and onto the road heading toward the Brenneman farm. The bishop's preaching always had a *gut* message that seemed to settle in her heart and brought her a little closer to *Gott* and His ways.

Her gaze roamed over the farms during the three-mile ride. It was a breath of fresh air to sit and enjoy the countryside around her. She held Leah on her lap and pointed at the chickens and the cows and the pigs, making their sounds each time.

Leah laughed. "Again, *Mamm*, again."

May stiffened. It was the first time Leah had called her *mamm* so clearly that the meaning finally sunk in. *Mamm*. Yes, she supposed she was the only *mamm* this little *mädel* would ever know. She hadn't thought about what hearing that word would be like. It was *wunderbaar*. She kissed Leah on the head as she practiced her animal sounds until she grew tired and leaned back against her.

May settled in to enjoy the rest of the short drive. She gawked at a neighbor's yard peppered with yellow chrysanthemums and white dahlias. Even their birdhouse had a new coat of paint. *Jah*, she would need to ask Thad to paint theirs, too. It was starting to look shabby. Two squirrels scampered around on the road bank, chasing each other, and she chuckled.

A wheel dropped in a pothole, and the buggy jerked, bouncing the seat and jiggling her closer to Thad. She could feel the heat from his body next to her. May caught her breath at his nearness. She held her gaze out the window and hoped the horse's hooves drowned out the pounding of her heart. Even though a cool breeze swirled through the buggy, she raised her hand and blotted the moisture from her forehead.

"You recieved a lot of orders and are bringing in a lot of money with the cheese business. I'm so proud of you, May. We won't have to worry next year where the seed money will come from or the money to repay the loan." Thad glanced her way and smiled.

"*Danki.* I do it for us, for Leah and to keep our farm."

"I know." He reached over, grabbed her hand and squeezed.

While Thad parked the buggy at the Brennemans' and talked to the men milling around the house, May carried Leah to a bench on the women's side and settled next to Janie. She rocked Leah back and forth until she fell asleep again.

After the singing of the *Loblied*, Preacher

David stepped to the front and gave the opening words, in Pennsylvania Dutch, to remind the congregation why it had gathered and called each member to humble their heart before *Gott*. When he concluded, May knelt with the others for silent prayer, then stood for the Scripture reading.

Preacher Paul delivered the main sermon, and May felt her heart open as the Holy Spirit worked His way in. When he finished, Bishop Yoder gave his testimony on denying thyself. *Jah*, he amazed her at his deep love for *Gott*.

The bishop cleared his throat before the reading of the banns. May smiled and often thought he did that as a little stalling tactic because he knew everyone loved to hear them.

"Now, I have a *wunderbaar* announcement. Elmer Plank and Josephine Bender will be married in four weeks."

May grabbed Janie's hand and whispered, "He asked Josie. I am so happy for them."

"Your cousin will be very happy. Elmer has a *gut* business and is a hard worker. And she will have a nice mother-in-law," Janie chuckled.

May nodded. "And Lois is a midwife so that will be handy."

Later on, they headed to the kitchen to help serve the common meal. Janie helped carry food out to the serving tables while May kept filling glasses with lemonade at the tables. She reached over Howard Lantz's shoulder to refill his drink as he remarked, "I might have to sell the farm."

A hush fell over the table.

"*Jah*, me, too," Tim Lambright said. "Milk prices are too low and the storm did a lot of damage."

May walked toward the end of the table where Jonah Hochstetler, Thad's youngest *bruder* who had already taken over the farm since he'd inherit it from Aaron and Gretchen someday, sat. "*Jah*, I'm in the same boat as all of you," Jonah confessed. "What with milk prices so low, the storm and losing some of this year's crop, I might lose *Daed*'s farm."

May watched the expression on Thad's face as he spoke to Jonah. "Why didn't you ask for a loan?"

"By the time I got to the Amish lenders, their money had run out. They said they would check with Indiana, but storms ripped through the whole Midwest. I could maybe get a regular loan but the interest would be so high I couldn't afford the payments." Jonah sipped his lemonade.

"What?" Thad stared at Jonah. "Why didn't you say something?"

"You have your own problems, Thad, but at least you have a *gut* woman to help you out."

May caught Gretchen's reaction as she set food on the table and glanced from *sohn* to *sohn*. It was a table full of men, so Gretchen would not interrupt them. But by the look on her face, it was the first time she'd heard that her youngest *sohn* might lose their family farm.

May could see the shock settle on her face as she turned pale and walked to the porch steps and sat.

"Thad, how is the new cheese business doing that you and May started?" Jonah asked, quickly changing the subject.

"It was the answer to our prayers, but May does most of the work. She took classes, studied hard and practiced the recipes. She learned all about making cheeses." Thad looked at May. "She has even gotten orders from some bigwig local real estate agent who likes to serve cheese and crackers at her fancy open houses. And she has other customers who give her weekly orders. Mr. Kolb has a gift shop. He made her a webpage and brings out her orders. May is very successful, aren't you?"

The table of men glanced her way.

"*Jah*, we are doing very well. But I only have two hands, well, four with Janie Conrad helping me. But the two of us can only handle so much business. We have too much business now so we are turning orders down. If your *frau* or *tochter* would like to help, we can take you into our business and share the profits."

The men at the table all started talking at once.

Thad held up his hand. "Wait a minute, May. Are you talking about taking on business partners?"

"I'm saying if the bishop doesn't want me to have a business, then all those who need extra money, if they want to contribute and help make cheese, they can share in the profits. It will be a community business."

"That's a *gut* idea, but if many want to help, our kitchen isn't big enough," Thad emphasized with a pointed look.

"They could make it in their own kitchen. Or maybe we could rent a building in town. It would keep us all busy," May offered.

She watched Jonah walk over to Janie and talk to her. She tried to inch closer, but she was still too far away to hear a word they said.

While May continued to pour lemonade, Thad canvassed the table to see how many were interested in taking part in their cheese business. When May poured Thad a glass of lemonade, he showed her the list he had put together.

"*Gut*, that means we can make more cheese," she said. "All those who want to learn the recipes and the tricks to making cheese will need to come or send their *frau* to our *haus* for training. What about Jonah, since he doesn't have a *frau*?"

Thad glanced at his *bruder*. "Jonah will supply more milk and cream, and he is *gut* at making ice cream. We could expand the business into yogurt and ice cream and maybe hire some *youngies* to help."

Jonah smiled and nodded in response to Thad. May noticed Bishop Yoder heading to the table. While the men gave it further discussion, she wandered over to the bishop. "What do you think of my idea, Bishop?"

"That's a fine idea. It's very generous

of you to share your knowledge, May, and make this a community project. That's what we are all about, community and thinking of others before ourselves."

"It's no different than a barn raising or helping someone with their crops when they have been sick. It's all about community service, *jah*?"

He smiled. "*Jah*, but it was nice that you offered to help teach the others."

May cleared the table when the men were through eating. Janie joined her, holding a big tub for the plates and cutlery that weren't disposable.

May set some serving bowls in the tub. "I saw Jonah talking to you. How did that go?"

"All right. It was hard talking to him. My heart was fluttering so badly. He just wanted to know how I was, and if I liked making cheese. Small talk."

May smiled. "*Jah*, I know. Just don't let him break your heart again."

Janie nodded. "I'll take this tub inside and come back."

When May finished wiping down the table, she turned toward the next table, but Gretchen was standing in her way.

"That was very nice of you to let others join in your cheese business, May." Her voice held a tone of humility; it was almost timid.

"It was the right thing to do. We are a community, *jah*? We help each other out."

"It must have taken hard work to learn the craft. It was thoughtful that you are willing to teach others. Maybe I will come over and help one day a week."

"That would be nice, Gretchen." May smiled and gave her a gentle pat on the arm. It was going to be easier being friends with her mother-in-law rather than not.

After the meal, May headed her buggy to her *onkel*'s farm only a mile away and parked by the other cousins already there. *Onkel* Thomas ran across the barnyard and helped her down. "You gave him a *gut* workout getting here after church," he laughed. "I'll brush him down a bit."

"*Danki, Onkel.*"

Aent Matilda met her at the door with a big hug. "You heard Josie is getting married in four weeks?"

"*Jah*, I'm so happy for her."

"Go upstairs and tell her. She expected you to drop by."

May ran up the stairs and knocked on Josie's bedroom door. "I'm really mad at you," she called from the hallway.

"Come in," Josie sang out.

May ran in and wrapped her arms around Josie, hugging her tight. "I'm so happy for you." She sat on the chair next to Josie and watched her work on her wedding dress.

"I was actually surprised when Elmer asked for that first buggy ride," Josie said.

"I think once he met you, Josie, he only had eyes for you."

Josie smiled. "*Danki* for stopping by."

"I'm going to let you sew in peace, and

head downstairs and see if your *mamm* has something for me to do."

Josie beamed with happiness.

May found *Aent* Matilda in the kitchen. "What would you like me to do?"

"I'm still making the list. Would you want to help me empty the hutch and set the *gut* china out for washing?"

May helped them until it was almost dark. Weary and alone, she and Tidbit made their way back home.

May was so happy for her cousin, but she couldn't help but wonder if she and Thad would ever be as happy. *Jah*, they'd become closer the past few weeks. But she still wasn't sure if Thad truly loved her.

Or if he ever would.

Chapter Sixteen

Thad heaved a sigh. He'd volunteered to take care of Leah today while May attended Monday's quilting frolic. He packed Leah's diaper bag, put her coat on and trudged across the yard to the *dawdi haus*. She coughed, fussed a bit rubbing her nose, then fell back to sleep on his shoulder. His *mamm* wanted to see Leah, and that would give him time to work in his *daed*'s wood shop.

The sharp October wind blew in his face as he carried her across the barnyard to the *dawdi haus*. The aroma of fresh brewed coffee was a pleasant welcome when he stepped into his parents' kitchen.

"Mornin'." His *daed* rushed to his side and grabbed Leah's bag. "A raw day to be out and about."

"*Gut* mornin'. I was wondering if *Mamm* could watch Leah for a bit while I work on some shelves in your workshop. May is at a frolic, and I volunteered to take care of Leah."

"Sorry, but your *mamm* is sick in bed with the flu. Probably not a *gut* idea to have Leah here."

"Sorry to hear that. Tell her I said to take care of herself." Thad hurried out the door. The short walk back seemed longer with Leah fussing and squirming.

She reared up, coughing and crying, as he hurried into the *haus*. He set her down, and slipped her out of her coat. Her little body was sweaty and all her clothes clung to her. He wiped her off, changed her and gave her some juice. She spit up the juice and pushed the cup away. When she fell asleep, he laid her in her downstairs crib. She woke up and cried. He picked her up and rocked her until she fell back to sleep. Later when he checked, she was very warm to the touch. He paced the floor as a shiver of fear crawled over his heart.

At 3:00 p.m., Thad heard a buggy pull into the drive. He peered out the window, then raced out the door to help May. "Leah is sick. You go in, and I'll unhitch Gumdrop."

May gasped and sprinted to Leah's crib. She laid a hand on her forehead and cheeks. They were burning.

Leah raised her head, her nose was running, but she smiled and held her arms out.

"*Hullo*, sweetie." May lifted the *boppli*, wrapped her in a hug and kissed her cheek.

Leah's breathing was wheezy and her chest rattled, but she snuggled close and laid her head on May's shoulder.

She waited for Thad to get back to the *haus*. "She's really sick. Call a driver. We need to take Leah to the hospital right away."

By the time he returned, Leah was quiet, too quiet. Her cheeks were red and her eyes glassy. Everyone was bundled and ready when the car arrived.

May was grateful for the warmth when she slid across the seat of the car. Thad set Leah in the middle and strapped her in the car seat. His quick actions helped May relax. The eighteen miles to the hospital in Iowa City seemed endless as she prayed.

When the car stopped at the emergency room entrance, Thad jumped out of the car and ran around to help May. *Gott* answered one prayer, there was no one ahead of them at the hospital admittance. As quickly as possible, a nurse took them to an examining room.

A few moments later, the door opened and a tall man in a white coat entered. He shook hands with Thad, then May. "I'm Dr. Evans. I'm the pediatrician on call. You're Mr. and Mrs. Hochstetler?"

Thad stepped forward. *"Jah."*

Dr. Evans's gaze jumped from Thad to May. "Tell me what's going on with Leah?"

May filled him in while the doctor examined her.

He ordered X-rays and several other tests. Then he left the room. After a while, he came rushing back in the exam room. "She's a very sick little girl. She has bacterial pneumonia. You're Amish?"

May nodded. *"Jah."*

"When Leah goes home, she needs to stay in the house as much as possible."

"Okay, for how long?"

"Preferably the rest of the winter. We don't want her catching pneumonia again."

"She's going to be all right then?" Relief washed over May.

"I'm admitting her for now. Her temperature is 103 degrees. She has an advanced infection. We need to monitor how she responds to the antibiotics. Has she ever been on antibiotics before?"

"Nein. No."

After they settled Leah in a crib, May

sat next to it and rubbed her back until she fell asleep. Tears filled May's eyes. Thad pulled up a chair and wrapped an arm around her. She settled into his embrace and laid her head on his shoulder.

The rest of the day they stayed with Leah only taking turns when they stretched their legs and got something to eat.

Monday evening, Thad left the room and came back with two blankets. He wrapped one around May, and he curled up in the chair next to the window.

She pulled the blanket tighter around her shoulders as the tears slid down her cheeks. If anything happened to Leah, it was her fault. While Leah had been sick, she'd traipsed off to the quilting frolic. May had wanted some time away with her friends. Now this little girl was in the hospital fighting for her life. Thad never said a word, he wouldn't. But her place was at home taking care of a sick *kind.*

Leah hadn't moved a muscle in a long time, and her breathing was still labored.

May stood and lightly laid her hand on the tiny back. Leah snuffled, moved her head back and forth but didn't wake. She drew in a deep ragged breath.

May woke during the night and stood at Leah's bed. She sounded a little better. Her sleep seemed more comfortable. Her cough sounded looser, and hopefully, the tightness in her chest was relaxing and the infection was starting to clear.

She needed to keep her promise to April and take care of Leah...and Thad.

Her sweet pumpkin still looked pale as a snowflake on a winter's day. Beautiful and unique like *Gott* made all his creations, yet fragile as a flower to remind May that she needed Him. Needed His grace and forgiveness for all her sins and for forgetting about Him except at times like this. May's heart swelled with the knowledge that *Gott* was beside her, helping her carry this burden.

When Thad took a walk, she pulled her Bible out of her quilted bag, turned to

Psalms and read. She had faith that Leah would fight off this infection and would return home soon with her and Thad. They were a family now and May realized she needed to work with Thad more to make that feeling strong. It wasn't her versus Thad. They had made the decision to marry and that was a lifetime commitment. She needed to honor that obligation. And if she would admit it to herself, the more time she spent with Thad, she felt safe and secure. By his side was the place she always wanted to be, beside him and Leah. Her family, a family that she never really had. Her *mamm* died young, her *daed* stayed busy, and she and April had differences. This was the first time she felt like she was really in a family.

Tuesday Morning, Thad woke and glanced at the clock on the hospital room wall. 5:00 a.m. He stretched and the aroma of coffee out in the hall awoke his mind and pried his eyes all the way open. Leah was quietly whimpering. She was probably hungry. He'd get a couple cups of coffee and tell the nurse.

May had finally drifted off to sleep. He'd woken during the night and heard her crying. She felt bad because she went to the frolic and blamed herself. He should have stayed home with Leah instead of dragging her over to his parents' *haus*. *Nein*, it was just as much his fault. If that wasn't bad enough, *Mamm* was sick and he'd exposed Leah to the flu.

Thad wiped away the moisture from his eyes. He opened the hospital room door a crack, squeezed through, got two cups of coffee and told the nurse—Dottie was her name—that Leah was waking up.

She nodded. "I'll be there in a minute."

When he went back to Leah's room, May was awake and sitting up and watching her. He handed May the coffee. Dark circles were like half-moons beneath her eyes. Her mouth pressed tightly into a straight line, and a tear was rolling down her cheek.

"We need the nurse," she whispered. "I've touched her cheek, and she's very hot."

"She's coming." He set his coffee down. "But I'll make sure." Before he reached the door, it opened and Dottie walked in.

She checked Leah and her fluids, took her temperature, and looked into her eyes and ears. Leah started to fuss. "I'm calling Dr. Evans," Dottie said at last. "Her temperature is up to 104 degrees." She rushed to the nurse's desk, leaving the door open. A minute later, she returned. "They're going to page the doctor. He's in the hospital making rounds."

The few minutes they waited seemed like an eternity. Finally the doctor ran into the room. He looked Leah over and listened to her heart. He ordered the nurse to start a new IV with a different antibiotic. She got the new bag, hung it and fiddled with the lines.

Dr. Evans glanced at Thad and May.

"She is not responding to this antibiotic. So we're going to try something else."

May threw her hand over her mouth as her body began to shake.

Thad wrapped both arms around her and held her tight. "Shh. Let the doctor work. Do you want to step out into the hall?"

"Nein," she said through gritted teeth.

Thad pulled May back toward the window and whispered in her ear, "We need to pray to *Gott*. That's how we must help the doctor and Leah."

May nodded, and he knew she was doing everything she could to prevent herself from crying. He placed his hands on her shoulders and pulled her to him. "Are you with me on this?"

"Jah."

"Heavenly Father, You took April and Alvin from us, please do not take Leah, too. She is so innocent. Please fill the doctor with the right knowledge, give him swift hands and a sharp mind. Please heal Leah, Father. Amen."

May stayed in Thad's embrace. He rested his cheek on the top of her head and held her tight.

Wednesday morning, May pulled the Bible from her bag and turned to 1 John 4:8-20 and read the scripture. Gott *is love...* Gott *is love. Hate has no part of Him.*

She bowed her head. Gott, *please forgive me for all the hateful thoughts I had toward April and Thad. I was jealous of April. I wanted what she had, but please don't take my foolishness out on Leah. Please save her, Father. Please heal her, Father* Gott. *Please don't take this little bit of sunshine from my life.*

May prayed and cried until a calm settled in her heart.

Thad sat next to her and wrapped an arm around her shoulders. He whispered in her ear, "*Jah,* she will get well. *Gott* will bless this little girl who has lost so much."

When Dr. Evans entered Leah's room he

asked the nurse to check Leah's temperature first.

The nurse flashed the results at the doctor. He nodded.

"The fever has started to come down. Her breathing should start to improve. The nurses' station has my number, and I'll stop back later to see how she's doing."

Thad nodded. "Thank you, Dr. Evans."

May tiptoed to the side of Leah's bed, and Thad stood by her side. Watching. Praying. And thanking *Gott*.

The rest of the day was a long one. May sat by Leah's bed for hours, staring at her. Drinking in her tiny face. Watching the movement of her fingers opening and closing as she slept, like she was grasping for something.

May rested her head in her hands and cried. If anything happened to Leah, it was her fault.

Thad sat next to her, wrapped an arm around her and whispered, "May, stop. Leah will get better. You're going to wake her. Let's go for a little walk down the hall, *jah*?"

She shook her head. "*Nein*, I don't want to leave her."

His voice was firm. "For one minute. You need to get up and walk."

"One minute," she repeated.

Dr. Evans returned Wednesday evening and examined Leah. "The fever is definitely coming down. Her breathing has improved, and she's started to respond to the new medication. She'll sleep a lot, so don't be alarmed at that. She needs the rest. It will help her body heal. I'll check her in the morning." He nodded to them and closed the door on the way out.

As soon as the doctor left, May felt Thad's arm relax on her shoulders, and she heard him sigh. She'd been selfish. Thad kept giving her comfort while his heart was breaking for his little *mädel*. She grabbed his hand and squeezed it. It seemed a vague attempt, but she was unsure how to comfort him.

Leah woke and smiled the minute she saw them. That frail little face warmed May. She picked her up and cuddled her warm body. After a few moments, she laid her back down in the crib.

"May, let's go for a walk and let Leah sleep," Thad suggested. "Or we could take turns and go on breaks to get food. Whichever you prefer."

"*Nein.* I can't leave Leah. She might need me."

Thad nodded that he understood and told her he'd get some food for them, returning as soon as he could.

Thad stepped back in the room from one of his walks and gave Leah a kiss. "I talked to the nurse. She said there were showers downstairs. If you wanted to freshen up."

May didn't take her eyes off Leah. "*Jah, datt* is *gut.* But I don't want to leave Leah just yet."

"I know." Thad leaned over and gave May a kiss on the forehead.

She didn't pull back. She might have almost liked it.

Early Thursday morning, Thad touched her on the shoulder. May opened her eyes to see him hovering over her. She glanced at the clock. She'd only slept a couple of hours. "Is something wrong with Leah?"

"*Nein.* The nurse said Leah's fever is down a little more and her breathing is much better. I have called a driver. He will take me home. I'll freshen up and bring you back clean clothes. Okay?"

"*Jah*, but don't be long."

Thad walked toward the door, turned and glanced over his shoulder. He winked as he closed the door. She tried to suppress a smile. Her heart raced at the little exchange and warmth flushed her cheeks. Did he just flirt with her?

When she glanced back at Leah, reality pinched her. Leah was April and Thad's *boppli*, not hers.

Why was it she could never get beyond that fact?

* * *

An hour after he left the hospital, Thad returned to Leah's hospital room. He walked to her crib, leaned down and kissed her head.

May tiptoed up behind him.

Thad wrapped his arm around her. "She's going to be fine. Leah is getting better hour by hour, and she's resting comfortably. Now you need to get some rest."

May stepped closer to him and laid her head on his shoulder. The touch of her hand rubbing his back was soothing. He felt like he could handle anything with her by his side.

He drew in a deep breath to slow his racing heart. Leah was resting. The color had started to return to her cheeks.

Still, if anything had happened to Leah, he never would have forgiven himself.

Gott, please forgive me. I am sorry for the burden this has placed on May. She feels responsible for Leah and me. Nein. *May has been hurt enough. None of this is her fault.* He raised his arm and wiped his shirtsleeve over his face.

"Thad? Thad? Are you all right?" May's voice grew louder.

"I'm fine." He reached over and folded May's hand in his, squeezing tight. His heart thumped so loud he was afraid she could hear. The more time he spent with May, the more he never wanted to leave her side.

She was his now, and he never wanted to let her go.

Chapter Seventeen

Five days later, Leah was finally home from the hospital and in her own crib. May smiled as she closed her pumpkin's bedroom door. She was still sleeping a lot, but the doctor said that was normal and essential for gaining her health back completely. May tiptoed down the stairs and started making breakfast.

Ten minutes later, Thad entered the kitchen. "Mmm, the bacon and eggs smell *gut*." He went straight for the table and sat down.

"*Gut* morning," May chirped. "You're a sleepyhead."

"With Leah safely home, I slept hard, awoke a new person, and thanked *Gott* for her recovery and that we're all together."

"*Jah*, feels *gut* to be home, but I was at the hospital so long and in a state of panic over Leah that I still feel anxious." And not just over Leah, but Thad. They had grown close in the hospital. How should she respond to him now?

"Are you still worried about Leah?" Thad asked.

"I'm heartbroken I didn't recognize the symptoms until they got so bad."

"Don't blame yourself. You're a first-time *mamm* and this was her first sickness. Anyone could have missed those signs. It came on all of a sudden."

"So you are not going to take any responsibility?" she huffed.

He jerked his head. "I… I didn't mean it like that. All I meant is, now we know more of what to look for when she has a sniffle. Check for a fever and listen to her breathing. We are *both* new parents, *jah*?"

May waved her hand in the air. "Never mind what I just said. You're right. I didn't mean any of that. It's as much my fault as any. I just felt like a failure that I went to that frolic, and I struck out at you."

"I know." His voice was sympathetic. "We'll both calm down and get our child-rearing confidence back in a few days."

While she cleared the table, he put on his coat and hat. "Later today, I've got a dairy association meeting. But I'll be in before I go. This meeting could take a while."

He strolled across the kitchen to the sink and stood next to May. He put a warm hand on her back. "We both need to forgive ourselves about not noticing earlier how sick she was." He slid his arm around her, leaned in and gave her a kiss on the cheek.

She could feel his closeness and hoped he couldn't hear her heart beating like an old windup clock. How could that be happening? How could her head know that he was completely wrong for her, yet her heart fluttered whenever he walked within six feet of her and looked forward to when he would come in at noon?

May couldn't wait for Thad to come in for lunch. She'd made his favorite, yumazuti, a goulash-type dish, with cherry pie for dessert. He deserved it for staying by her side when Leah was sick.

Her heart fluttered when he walked through the door and flashed her a big smile. Where he was concerned, she had trouble thinking in terms of *liebe. Jah,* she cared for Thad. More and more. But she found herself tamping down her feelings until they were hidden.

He had tossed her aside the minute April smiled his way. Now she had to remember this was a marriage of convenience and that was all. He'd never really said he loved her.

"*Danki* for making the yumazuti, it is *gut,* but not as *gut* as this pie. You spoil me. How is Leah?"

"She was up for a little while. She lingered over breakfast, not much of an appetite. She played with Blackie and her doll for a while, now she is back in bed napping. Her cheeks are rosy again, just not a lot of pep."

Thad patted her on the shoulder after lunch. "Spend your day with Leah and let everything else go."

She nodded. He walked to the door, opened and closed it in a hurry so only a small draft of cool air found its way into the kitchen.

After cleaning the kitchen, she slipped upstairs and checked on Leah. The little girl lifted her head off the crib mattress and gave May a big smile, holding herself up with her arms. *Jah*, she was indeed getting stronger.

May picked her up and sat in the rocker. Leah leaned against her. Blackie sneaked in through the open door and jumped up on May's lap. Leah giggled and petted the kitten.

"Here, kitty." She patted her leg and wanted him on her lap.

"Leah, you are my little bit of sunshine." May kissed the top of her head and smelled her apple-blossom taffy-colored hair.

Leah pulled at her *kapp* strings, patted her face, then leaned forward and placed a big kiss on May's mouth.

May chuckled. "You are feeling better. *Datt* is the first kiss I've gotten in days."

Leah clapped her hands together and giggled. Her dark blue eyes and perfectly arched brows were the exact image of Thad. He was handsome, and Leah was a delicate little doll, like April.

May hugged Leah and whispered, "Every time I look at you, I'll never forget who your parents are." She kissed Leah's cheek. "But I do *liebe* you, precious little one. You have stolen my heart for always." She squeezed and hugged her little morsel again. "It is time you ate, little one, then you can play with your blocks while I do a few things."

May hadn't been fair to Leah, Thad or herself. She had married him for the wrong reason. Leah deserved a *mamm* and *daed* who could show love and affection for each other as well as for Leah. Thad said that he loved May, but she knew that it wasn't true. He only needed a *mamm* for Leah.

May kissed the *boppli* on the cheek. "Sorry, little one, that I got caught in the past. We better get to work."

While Leah sat on the kitchen floor, banging her building blocks, May gathered her canning kettle, leftover jars and utensils, carted them to the pantry and set them on the top shelf for winter. The rest of the day was spent catching up on laundry and other work that she'd pushed aside while staying at the hospital. For supper, she fried potatoes and pork chops, then set them on a warming plate.

Thad stomped through the kitchen door and rushed in panting. "Sorry, I'm in a hurry. Dairy association meeting. I forgot."

"Supper is ready. Do you have time to eat?"

"*Jah.* Just a few minutes. I'll wash up quickly."

They sat at the table, bowed their heads for silent prayer, then dug in.

"You're quiet." She finished filling Leah's bowl, set a spoonful of potatoes on her plate and took a bite.

"*Jah*, I'm anxious to see if there is a new development. There is some kind of rumor about a letter. I'm anxious to get there and see what's going on." Anxiousness laced his words.

He glanced up from his meal and locked eyes with her. Worry pulled his mouth into a taunt line. "I'm not sure what's going on. The big ranchers keep producing more and more milk and will soon infringe on our smaller markets. They produce faster and cheaper. Our milk is organic from grazed cows, which makes the amount produced less, but it's better quality. I think tonight they want to talk about reducing the price…again." His voice was strained.

"We could expand the business, but after Leah's illness, I had hoped to spend more time with her."

"*Nein.* You take care of Leah and make cheese as you have been. The cheese-making was only to help out, not to be a full-time job for you."

"I haven't been making cheese at all since Leah's been sick. I could always take in sewing this winter."

The color in Thad's cheeks heightened. "*Nein,* not unless you really want to do that. But I don't want Leah to be out in the cold if a *youngie* can't come to the *haus* and watch her." He shot her a warning look. Then he stood up and walked out the door.

May hadn't meant to upset him, and she knew he had a lot on his mind. A twinge twisted in her gut. She wasn't helping him enough. She'd make more rag rugs and maybe work on a quilt while Leah slept.

She could get quite a bit of money for a large quilt, slightly less for a *boppli* or youth quilt.

She glanced at the door Thad had gone out. They were a team. And they had to figure out how to save their farm together. But she could certainly think up more ideas to discuss with him…

Thad tapped the reins on Tidbit's back. "Come on, *bu,* it's not bedtime yet, you still got work to do."

Tidbit stepped out smartly and the trip to the dairy association meeting went quickly. When he got there, he pulled up the reins and parked his buggy next to all the others.

The meeting and discussion had already started. *Jah,* he was late and shouldn't have eaten supper. He quietly weaved between rows of chairs and stepped over feet to find an empty chair.

The president tapped a mallet on the table. "We need a show of hands on the suggestion to write a letter to the USDA about tightening the regulations."

An Amish man from the other side of the room shouted, "We *have* to write the letter. The big producers from out west have flooded the market with what they call 'organic milk' but there is much doubt that it all meets the organic grazing standard. The USDA needs to ensure stricter inspection criteria so all the organic milk meets the standard. The overproduction means we have to sell some of our organic at regular price or we'll go broke."

A second man behind Thad shouted, "Another dairy farmer in Wisconsin had to sell his farm."

Thad stood. "*Jah*, I agree. We have to send the letter. Our prices keep falling. The word *organic* must be stated clearly as grass-fed, during the grazing season." He sat down and leaned back in his chair while others said their piece.

The talking and debating went on for another hour before the mallet hit the desk and they finally took the vote.

It was late and Thad was bone-weary by the time he made it home. May had left the flashlight by the door so he could find his way to the bedroom in the dark. But he already knew sleep wouldn't come easy tonight. It wasn't just the milk he was worried about.

He was worried about May, too.

Chapter Eighteen

Thad stepped into the house and dropped down into a chair in the family room. Exhaustion and worry pulled at every bone in his body. The farm was losing money by the day. He scrubbed a hand over his face and ran it down his beard.

His mind kept wandering to thoughts of May standing at the sink in her blue dress. An image of her, with little auburn tendrils at her temples touching her cheek and teasing her smoky gray eyes, sent his heart beating faster.

Sleep tugged at his eyelids and pushed him out of the chair. He trudged up the steps to the second floor. Stopping to peek in on Leah, he saw May asleep in the rocking chair, her feet pulled up and scrunched under her afghan.

He removed his shoes and padded down the hall in his stocking feet. After a wide yawn, he hurried and got ready for bed, snuggled deep into the mattress, and covered with the quilt May had made him when she saw how tattered his was, then let his head sink into the softness of the pillow.

The ringing of the clock startled him. He bounded out of bed. The cold floor coaxed his feet into a dash across the room to retrieve his clothes and return to the warmth of the rag rug May had made.

A stream of daylight pulled his attention to the window. The sky was clear and the sun rose big and yellow, glowing like a bonfire chasing away the darkness.

He hurriedly dressed, and tiptoed past Leah's room, carrying his shoes in his hands. During the night, he'd heard May up twice trying to comfort Leah, cranky and still recovering from her illness.

The smell of hot maple syrup greeted him the second he entered the kitchen. Pancakes. His favorite. Plus May had opened a mason jar of canned peaches. He made a beeline to the table like a dog with his nose in the air. "Mornin'."

"*Gut* morning. How'd your meeting go last night?"

"We voted to send a letter to the USDA."

"Do you think it will help?"

He poured syrup on his hot stack of pancakes. "Can't hurt. Sorry, a lot on my mind."

"I know."

He let his eyes wander over May as she stood at the stove. Trying to ignore his feelings for her, he dropped his gaze back to his plate, and took another bite. After draining the last sip of coffee from the cup, he blotted the drip that dribbled down his chin. He eyed the remaining stack of pancakes on the platter. *Nein*, time to get busy. He pushed his chair from the table and stood.

"Would you like another stack?"

"*Nein.* Chores are waiting." He finger-combed his hair back, plopped his hat on, then shrugged into his coat.

The sound of wheels crunching over the frozen ground came closer and stopped by the house. Thad peered out the window, then darted out the door to the porch. "Caleb, what brings you out so early?"

"I wanted to get your thoughts on last night's meeting," Caleb said. "You look tired this morning. Didn't sleep well after listening to all that debating last night?"

"*Nein*, I got some sleep, but not much." Thad was silent for a moment, then blurted out, "I asked Bishop Yoder to play match-maker for me and May, like you suggested, and press her into marrying me, but instead of a *frau*, I have a nanny and…*nein*, I didn't mean that. I'm just tired. I wanted to talk to May last night and bounce some ideas off her after the dairy association meeting, but she is always fussing over Leah."

May heard Thad and Caleb talking on the porch and noticed the door ajar. She set the dish she was washing on the counter, reached for the door and heard her name. She listened and clutched at her chest.

Thad sent the bishop to pressure me to marry him? She stumbled to a chair. Of all the cruel things Thad had done to her, this was the worst. He thought her life was that trivial that he could dictate whom she married? She'd trusted her heart to him once again, and once again he'd betrayed that trust.

The burning on her cheeks lasted all the way upstairs. She poked her head into Leah's room to check if she was asleep. May quietly ducked into her room, pulled her suitcase out from under the bed and heaved it on top.

Thad had not only ruined her life once before, she let him into her heart, and he'd ruined her life again. She couldn't get a divorce, but she didn't have to live with him. Her body shook with sobs until her knees buckled, crumbling her to the bed. She let the grief drain from her soul.

After several minutes, she gathered her strength, pushed off the bed and packed her suitcase. *Nein.* He would not betray her trust again. She loved Leah and always would, but she could not stay with a man that had that little regard for her.

This was the last time that he would make a fool out of her. She wandered to the window and let her eyes feast on the red buildings surrounded by the white picket fence, the large garden area and the cows grazing in the pasture. A sight she'd probably never see again once she moved to Shipshewana.

She'd never come back. And never see her *daed*'s farm, the one she'd grown up on, ever again.

Squeezing her eyes closed, she turned from the *wunderbaar* view. Since she wouldn't be coming back to this *haus* again, she'd need to find everything she wanted and have it sent to *Aent* Edna's. There were a few of her mother's things in the attic that she'd like to take with her. The walnut whatnot shelves that *Grossdaddi* made *Mamm*. After April and Thad married, April put away several of *mamm*'s mementos so she could give the *haus* her own personal touch. If there was anything remaining after May left, she would tell Thad it should go to Leah.

She took her dresses off the hangers, folded them as neatly as she could with her hands shaking like a kite in the wind, and placed them in the suitcase. She'd never imagined that Thad would treat her with such a cold heart.

Hurrying around the *haus*, she gathered boxes and the belongings she had to have, then packed them for the three-hundred-mile trip to Shipshewana. She closed the box lid and hesitated. The finality of her actions spun around in her head as she glanced around the kitchen. If she moved out, she'd never return.

The screen door opening startled May. She jumped out of the pantry so fast it reminded her of the time *Mamm* had caught her dipping into the cookie jar between meals.

Thad stuck his head through the crack in the door. "I'm going over to Caleb's to help him with some work. I'll be back for supper."

"Okay." May blew out the breath she held as the door banged closed.

Leah let out a cry. May left the box in the pantry, poured a cup of milk from the refrigerator and took it upstairs.

Leah stopped crying as soon as May entered the room, her little mouth turning into a sweet smile.

"Oh, *datt* is such a charming face, it chased away all those big tears."

Leah laughed and smiled again, batting her lashes.

"Yes, you will be a heartbreaker like

your *mamm* so your *daed* better keep a close eye on you, for sure and for certain."

May sat in the rocker while Leah sipped her cup of milk and fiddled with May's dangling prayer *kapp* strings, her deep-blue eyes big with mischief. She grasped the strings and let go, grasped and let go, then batted them back and forth with a fist.

"So you found a new toy, huh?"

Leah smiled like she understood every word May said. When she finished her milk, they played with the blocks on the floor.

A lump grew in May's throat. How was she ever going to leave this child? She carried her downstairs, put her in her high chair and gave her the blocks. "And don't be tossing them off the tray."

May's heart was splitting in two. Stay or go? But how could she stay? She pulled a hanky from her pocket and blotted the tears streaming down her cheeks. Her grief tucked away, she stood at the stove and browned the stew meat, then cut up potatoes, onions and carrots. She let it all simmer in a big pot.

While Leah played, May packed a few more things. With the *kind* watching, it made boxing up her things very difficult.

After a few hours, Leah's eyes couldn't stay open. Ever since her pneumonia, she wore out earlier than usual. May fed her, tucked her into her crib for the night and returned to the kitchen.

When she heard Thad's buggy in the drive and go to the barn, she dished up the stew and waited. When Thad entered, he hung his coat, washed up and joined her at the table.

They sat and bowed their heads for silent prayer.

"It's cold out there," Thad said at last. "Wouldn't be surprised if we have snow soon."

"I imagine so, it's late fall." She took her fork and stirred it around in her stew.

"Is something wrong? You seem quiet."

May took a deep breath. "I heard you

talking to Caleb today on the porch. Is it true? You went to see Bishop Yoder and had him press me for an answer? And tell me people were talking about me when that wasn't really true? You tricked me, forced me into marrying you so I could take care of your nanny problem. You told him I was the best person for the job."

His jaw dropped.

"You trapped me in a loveless marriage?"

At first, Thad couldn't believe it. How could he convince her of the truth?

"May, please believe me. I *liebe* you."

"I can't believe you went to Bishop Yoder. You lied to me about everything. Everything, Thad. My whole life with you was a lie. I'm leaving and moving to Indiana. You'll need to find a real nanny for Leah."

"You can't leave! We're married," he said.

She raised her chin. "Yes, I can, and you

can't stop me. I've had it with you and your lies. Tell the bishop that."

"What about Leah? She'll miss you so much."

Her voice caught. "I'll miss Leah, but she's little and will soon forget me. I can't stay with you, Thad. I can't forgive you this time. You've gone too far. I'm all packed. I'll find a place to stay here in town until I can catch the train to Shipshewana."

His voice turned raspy. "I'll take Leah over to *Mamm*'s tomorrow. We can stay in the *dawdi haus* for a few days until you can move. But I'd like to try to work this out, May. I do truly *liebe* you. I don't want you to go."

"I'm boxing up what I want, and the rest can go to Leah. I'll let you know when I'm leaving."

May walked out of the room—and out of his life.

Chapter Nineteen

The next morning, Thad hurried to pack a bag while May gathered Leah's belongings. The mood in the *haus* was tense, and he needed to get away so he could think clearly, figure out what his next steps should be.

He carried their things out to the buggy, then came back inside for Leah. He'd take Leah over to his parents' *dawdi haus* on Jonah's farm for the night. "I'll come back and do the chores, but I won't come in the *haus*. I won't bother you any longer than need be." The words stuck in his throat and nearly choked him.

He'd never meant to hurt her. How could he make her understand that? How careless of him to even bring the subject up to Caleb. He felt like kicking himself. They had started their union with a marriage bargain. He should have been more sensitive, more careful.

She nodded. "It's your *haus* and your food. You can come in and eat."

Nein. He knew she couldn't stand the sight of him. "We'll call it quits right here. No more contact, no more uncomfortable moments or forced talking to be nice."

She shrugged.

His brain was too tired to figure out what that meant. The only thing he wanted was to get out of here. His heart felt like it was ripped out and dragged around like a piece of dirt. Sadness, bitterness, loneliness all washed through his body at once.

Gott, *I only did what You asked. I asked You to guide my steps and look where it has gotten me.*

He needed to get away. To put some

distance between him and May. When he tried to step in the buggy, Tidbit paced the ground and jiggled the buggy. "Whoa. Whoa." He walked over, laid a hand on Tidbit's neck and stroked it. "*Jah*, big guy, I know you sense my tension, and you don't like it."

The horse calmed at his soothing voice. Finally, Thad stepped into the buggy and set Leah on his lap. He tapped Tidbit's reins and the buggy lurched ahead as the horse started to move.

In a few minutes, the motion of the buggy had Leah fast asleep. Thad glanced down at her face and sighed. He swiped away the tears rolling down his cheeks, then gazed out the window at the frozen ground, the harvested fields, the dead grass. Jah, Gott, *I get it. It's winter and time to let the ground rest and let my soul rest. Maybe I should have been honest with May instead of stacking lie upon lie.*

He'd had two marriages in eighteen months. He felt burned-out. Tired. He'd tried to *liebe* April as best he could, and he did *liebe* May with his whole heart and soul. Maybe his calling in life was just to raise Leah.

May was hurting. He got that, but he'd hoped she cared about him enough to forgive him. But *nein*, that was not going to happen. Tomorrow he'd go see Bishop Yoder and ask if it was possible, if he'd make a special exception and let him and May get a divorce. Their marriage was never going to work.

After a twenty-minute ride to Jonah's farm, he parked the buggy, carried Leah in, still sleeping, and laid her in the crib his parents had set up especially for their *Enkelin*.

He drew a deep breath, then found his *mamm* sitting in the kitchen and told her everything.

"Thaddaeus Thomas Hochstetler, you go back to that *haus* and make up with May right now! She is a *gut* woman and a hard worker. You hurt her feelings."

"I didn't mean it. I was tired."

"That is no excuse."

Thad sighed and looked down at his shoes. "*Jah*, you're right, *Mamm. Danki.*"

The next morning, he begrudgingly got himself out of bed, dressed Leah and asked his *mamm* to watch her while he drove to town.

Thad stepped out of the buggy in front of the bishop's *haus*. The door burst open and the bishop appeared, signaling him to enter.

"Morning, Bishop Yoder."

"You're out early and on such a bitty morn." The bishop steered Thad into the kitchen. "Rebecca, if there is coffee left, would you fetch us a couple of cups?"

"*Gut* morning, Thad, so nice to see you." She ran to the kitchen, then came back out with two cups of coffee. She set them down, and discreetly disappeared into another room. No doubt a prearranged courtesy when the bishop had visitors.

"So, what can I do for you this morning, Thad? You're already happily married."

"*Jah*, about that… May found out that I tricked her into marrying me and she is angry. Very angry. So angry she's leaving me."

"Thad, slow down, you're making no sense. What has happened?"

"May found out that I sent you to talk to her, to insist that we marry. She loves Leah like her own *kind*, and I thought it would work out. But she doesn't trust me or believe anything I say now, and I fear she never will. I broke her heart not just once, but twice. She wants to live apart, but that's not fair to her. I want to set her free. I want a divorce."

The bishop's eyes widened. "Thad, you know that is forbidden among us."

"I know, but since we just got married a few months ago, I thought you could make an exception somehow." He tried to send the bishop a pleading look.

"*Nein.* Absolutely not. Your request can't

be approved. You'll need to work it out, you and May," the bishop said firmly.

"She doesn't want to live with me. May can't get past how much I hurt her." Thad's voice turned earnest.

The bishop folded his hands together on top of the table. After a silent moment, he spoke softly. "Yours is the first match I have made where the couple wants a divorce. I may have to throw away my matchmaking hat after this." He tried to lighten the air. "I hope this foolishness doesn't get around."

Thad was in no mood to listen to a joke.

The bishop patted the table twice with his hand, scooted his chair back and stood. "Let me take your situation under consideration. No one has ever complained before. Give me a few days."

"Bishop, May wants to buy a train ticket and move to Shipshewana as soon as she can."

"Why, that's nonsense! Why would she want to do that? What about Leah? She needs a *mamm*." Bishop Yoder headed for the door.

Thad stopped in the doorway. "Because she hates me and wants to get as far away from me as possible."

The bishop lightly put his hand on Thad's shoulder, turned him around and pushed him out the door. The door closed firmly behind him.

Thad rubbed his chest. He already missed May, and she wasn't even gone yet. What would happen when she left Iowa for *gut*?

May trudged up the stairs, trying not to spill the bucket of water or the cleaning caddy she carried. She turned the knob, opened the attic door and gasped as a huge cobweb hit her in the face. She set the bucket down and wiped the cobweb off her mouth. The air smelled dusty and stale, as she batted a hand to circulate some fresh air. Dabbing a rag in the water, she wrung it out and wiped around the doorframe to remove other webs and dirt.

She turned the flashlight on and shone the beam around, grateful the bishop let them use the device when necessary. She held the light in front of her as she stepped through years of accumulated dust.

From one end of the attic to another sat old furniture, objects of many treasured memories. Things she had long forgotten about: lamps, shelves and boxes marked *Mamm*, April or *grosseldre*. A pang of longing touched her heart.

She sighed deeply. It'd take her a month to sort through this mess. Her footfalls echoed on the wood flooring as she walked through the maze of cartons and old dressers. She moved a stack of boxes and stared… April's oak *boppli* cradle. *Daed* had carved a fancy design on the head and footboard. May took the wet rag, wiped it down and cleaned the top edge where the name was carved. APRIL.

Her eyes filled with tears. It was as

beautiful as her sister. She straightened and flashed the light all around. Where was her cradle? If her memory was correct, hers was plain with no carving on it. Finally she saw it, sitting farther back. She pushed a box of toys out of the way, picked up the dusty cradle and carried it to a cleared spot.

She dipped the rag in the bucket of water, wiped off a layer of years and flashed the light over the cradle. Astonished, she stepped back. It was made of a dark brown walnut. Plain, yes, but lovely inside and out. Carving would have destroyed the natural beauty of the wood.

Nein. Was that really her old cradle? She dipped the rag in the water and wiped a spot on the top edge. MAY.

She finished cleaning it and set the cradle with the other things she wanted to keep. May flashed the light around again and uncovered a big object that had been sitting next to April's cradle. *Mamm*'s oak buffet. Beside that, she saw *mamm* and *daed*'s bedroom set. What was it doing here?

May huffed. Thad, of course. Something as *wunderbaar* as this bedroom set and that buffet, he hid away in the attic for the rodents to run across and gnaw on with their teeth.

Thad and April must have moved them up here on a day when May wasn't home. Since *Mamm* died, they didn't have large family dinners anymore. She had forgotten all these treasures were even here.

Tears welled up in her eyes as she drew in a ragged breath. She wouldn't be able to take any of these things to *Aent* Edna's *haus*. She couldn't afford to ship all this. And even if she could, there would be no space for these things there.

May stumbled back against the buffet, her body shaking in uncontrollable sobs. She wasn't just leaving Thad, she was leaving her family and all that she loved. Leah would never know what any of this was, who it belonged to, or what it represented. She'd never know her *mamm* or her *grosseldre.*

May calmed herself and dried her tears.

After dusting the top of the dresser, May set her rag down and opened a drawer. It wasn't empty...it was stuffed full of dresses. *Mamm*'s things? But she'd given all *Mamm*'s clothing to a woman who had lost everything in a *haus* fire. They must have missed these. Well, she could tear them up into strips and weave them into rag rugs.

May picked up one of the dresses and shook it out. A spiral-bound notebook dropped to the floor. She bent, retrieved the book held closed by a blue ribbon and laid it on top of the dresser. She held up the dress. This would never have fit *Mamm*'s stout frame. *Mamm* had loved her strawberry-filled jelly donuts every morning and pie for supper. Whose dresses were they?

She glanced at the spiral-bound book. She folded the dress, slipped it back in the drawer, closed it and lightly caressed the book with her fingertips before picking it up. She had never seen *Mamm* write in such a book. Maybe it was her recipe book. After she'd died, May hadn't been able to find it.

Wait a minute! She opened the drawer again, grabbed a dress and held it up. These weren't *Mamm*'s. They were April's before she got pregnant. She must have stored her old clothes in *Mamm*'s dresser.

A chill swept over May like the wind skimming over the pond on a cool evening. She picked up the notebook, untied the blue ribbon and slowly started to open the cover, then snapped it closed and threw it back on the dresser.

She stared at the book. What if it contained love letters to Thad? She choked back a tear and swallowed hard. *Nein.* She didn't want to read April's passionate words to Thad. And maybe his letters to her were inside.

She flopped in the chair, her heart racing. The pain from April and Thad's betrayal still stabbed at her chest.

Why had May ever married Thad? She could never get a divorce, and the reminder of his *liebe* for her own sister stared her in the face every day when she looked at Leah. The *kind* had April's face and Thad's dark blue eyes.

Maybe it was best for everyone if she did move to Shipshewana. *Why,* Gott, *after everything I've been through all my life living in April's shadow, did You allow this to happen to me?*

She noticed the blue ribbon dangling over the edge of the dresser. May grabbed the book. She didn't want to see April's words professing her love for Thad, but she needed closure.

She flipped the cover open and scanned the words...

Dear Diary—

Her heart raced. It was definitely April's writing. Did she really want to know what April had hidden away from prying eyes?

Something that was personal to her and no one had a right to see…

May needed to know the truth. *Had* to know the truth. She gingerly flipped the page.

Alvin and I *liebe* each other so much we can hardly stand to be apart. We sneak out at night to meet down at the creek and lie in each other's arms until almost dawn. We talk for hours and plan our future.

May's hand shook as she turned the page. With each page, she devoured word after word, paragraph after paragraph, that spoke of April's love, but not for Thad, for Alvin, Thad's older *bruder*.

I'm pregnant! Alvin and I are so happy. We can't wait to marry and share our lives with our *boppli*. This is the happiest time of my life. The bishop will read our banns on Sunday.

She scanned down the page and stopped…

My life is a total shambles and my heart is breaking. Alvin died in a buggy accident. It's just the *boppli* and me. *Danki*, Alvin, for giving me a small part of you; I will treasure this gift always. The bad part is…when they know I'm pregnant, and as members of the church, they will shun the *boppli* and me.

Her hand flew to her chest as May read on.

Thad has volunteered to marry me so the *boppli* can have a name and the community won't shun us. I feel awful but I hope that someday May can forgive me. I'm desperate and have no place else to go.

May read for hours. About Thad, how his and Alvin's *daed* made Thad marry April to keep her and the *boppli* from a shunning. At last, May burst into tears. Thad gave up his own life for his brother, April and Leah. Thad had chosen to sacrifice his happiness for the rest of the family.

Her heart sunk to the floor as her tears drenched her cheeks. She crumpled back in the chair, wiping her eyes and face with her hanky. Thad was an honorable man. He had kept April and Alvin's secret all this time.

Now that she and Thad had separated, his *liebe* for her, like an old relic set in the attic and forgotten, would soon turn to dust.

Chapter Twenty

The sun peeking through the window shone a warm beam on May's face and roused her from a restless sleep. Her mind sputtered to life after only a few hours of sleep, then began to focus. She regretted lying awake half the night rehearsing what she'd say to Thad. The thought of seeing him pushed her out of bed and hurried her to dress.

While the oatmeal cooked, she kept rehearsing what she'd say to him. She'd start by apologizing. Surely he'd understand. He had only moved out a few things so it wouldn't take long to move back.

She selected her dark blue dress to wear. It deepened the color of her eyes, he once said.

Her hands shook when she slipped the harness on Gumdrop and tightened the girth. Words and phrases danced around in her head. How was she going to apologize to Thad? Would he ever forgive her?

She tapped the reins against Gumdrop. "Giddyap." The horse trotted down the drive, past the garden, onto the road, and increased his gait as he passed the white picket fence. It was only a twenty-minute ride to Jonah's farm and his parents' *dawdi haus*.

May relaxed back in the seat, but the closer she rode to the Hochstetler farm, the faster her heart beat. Her palms were damp. It was like the first time Thad had asked her to go on a buggy ride. He'd been nervous and his tongue had stumbled over the words. All she'd been able to reply was *jah*.

Her chest squeezed her ribs so hard she could barely breathe.

She urged Gumdrop into a faster trot. May's heart raced, thinking about throwing herself into Thad's arms. She could feel his arms around her right now, pulling her closer for a kiss.

Her stomach turned somersaults.

"Hurry, Gumdrop, hurry." She took a deep breath and exhaled slowly. *Lord* Gott, *danki for setting me straight. I should have believed Thad all along.*

She'd surprise him with...what? Her newfound forgiveness because now she knew the truth? Would he be insulted because she hadn't trusted and believed him?

Another thing spun around in her head. Why hadn't he just told her about what was going on? Why did he feel the need to keep it a secret? Maybe he really had loved April.

She would never know for sure, but she had to trust Thad.

A tug to the right on the reins turned

Gumdrop into the drive. She guided his steps to the *dawdi haus* around to the back of the main *haus*. Drawing a deep breath, she blew it out and stepped down.

May knocked on the door. No answer.

She knocked again and stepped back. This time she heard footfalls in the hall on the other side of the door.

The door opened and Thad motioned for her to enter. "Did you come to see Leah?"

"*Nein.* I was hoping she'd be asleep. I need to talk to you."

He led the way to the sitting room. "Have a seat."

He sat on a chair next to the heating stove opposite the couch, his glance darting everywhere, avoiding eye contact with her. His actions made her uncomfortable, but she didn't blame him after the way she'd treated him.

"Thad, I found April's diary, and I know what you did and why."

He was silent for a moment. "So what are you saying? Now you forgive me and everything is okay?" His manner was strangely calm. "You've forgotten about the past and that April and I were married?"

Her heart skipped a beat. What was he saying? She wanted it to work, she really did. She loved him… But she hadn't thought about if she had fully forgiven him. Had she really turned her back on what he'd done to her? All she'd really found out was that April hadn't loved Thad, and Thad hadn't loved April.

At least she didn't think so. Confusion stirred inside her.

Thad's eyes locked with hers. "Sometimes people just aren't meant to be together. People don't usually flip from hate to love overnight. I ruined your life—twice. I'm sure now, after reading April's diary, you want to forgive me. The thing is, you can't just want to. You have to do it. And in this case, it also means that you have to forgive me for marrying April and all that went along with that choice."

"I've loved you all my life, Thad."

He crossed the room, sat by May and placed his hands on her shoulders, and turned her toward him. "*Jah*, even when I was married to April? You realize if your sister hadn't died, we'd still be married."

May's heart felt like it had just been punched. "Why are you saying this to me?"

"I can read it in your eyes. Your heart loves me and has forgiven me...but your head is saying stay away from him."

His words stabbed her. She hadn't really thought it all through.

He patted her hand with his large, calloused palm. "I've asked the bishop to let us divorce."

"He'll never grant that. Amish can't divorce."

"Let's wait and see."

"You and Leah could come back and live at the *haus*." She wrung her hands in her lap.

"*Nein.* I think it's better that we are apart

right now, and that we don't confuse Leah too much. *Mamm* is going to watch her for a few days. Let's each take some time away from each other. You could even go to Shipshewana like you've always talked about. Maybe then you could decide where you want to live. Edna wanted to leave the café to you if you'd move out there. That is a *gut* opportunity for you. She has no other close heirs and wants you to work with her."

He didn't want her.

He removed his arm from her shoulders.

Her heart had already told her where she wanted to be. She got up and walked to the door.

Thad followed. "May, it's for the best. I can see the distrust in your eyes. Your heart might want me, but that's not enough. No matter how much you think you want this. I want you to *liebe* me and to accept all that I am, including my flaws and the choices I made in the past, whether they were good or bad."

The heat from the stove and her jangled nerves made it hard to breathe. "*Jah.* We'll talk later." She reached for the doorknob, but Thad got it first and opened the door.

"I'll walk you out."

"*Nein.* I'm okay. Stay in here with Leah."

Gumdrop was waiting in the drive. He stomped his feet, snorted and shook his head when she approached. *Jah,* she felt that same way.

She rubbed a hand down Gumdrop's nose, then put her arms around his neck and gave him a hug. "I want someone to *liebe,* so it looks like you're stuck with the job." His sympathetic big brown eyes looked at her. "You have *gut* intuition."

She climbed in and tapped the reins on his back. "Let's skedaddle, big boy. I feel a *gut* cry coming on." He took off as if promised a big bucket of oats.

She turned him onto the road, and urged him into a faster trot. The fence posts flashed by and field after harvested field disappeared as Gumdrop flew down the road.

Her heart felt like those fields...picked clean.

A knife stuck in his heart when May walked out the door. She was the air that he breathed. He didn't want to let her go, but this time he needed to do what was best for her. For them. Thad could tell by May's eyes when she spoke about finding April's diary that it was more a matter of she *wanted* to believe. Not what she actually *did* believe.

Thad wandered through the *haus*. What had he done? He knew he'd been selfish to have married her, he should have waited, but *nein*, his heart had ruled over his head and all reasoning had fled. What was he thinking of to put her through it again? Her eyes held a sadness that cut to his core.

He had to be the dumbest man on earth when it came to women.

When Leah awoke, he fed her, then left

her with his *mamm* while he attended the dairy meeting.

He shuffled around three men sitting at the end of a row, and sat next to Caleb. He plunked down on the chair as if he didn't really want to be there.

Caleb eyed him. "Is everything okay? I drove by your place and saw you carrying out some suitcases."

"It's nothing to worry about." He stared straight ahead. He wasn't ready to explain it to Caleb or anyone else.

As they called the meeting to order, he had to shake the image of May from his head.

The president of the dairy association stood wearing a somber face and waved a letter that Thad could see had the USDA logo. The president wasn't smiling. Thad's heart nearly stopped. The dairy was a big part of his livelihood. The knife plunged deeper and twisted. No doubt, that reply was going to mean he'd lose business on his dairy cows. They had the co-op cheese business that May started, but now he had no *frau* to make his cheese and sell it.

Finally, a smile broke out on the president's face. "The USDA has agreed to review the information brought to them regarding the big producers violating the organic rules. The letter also states the USDA inspection agency would write a citation to those producers who knowingly violate the regulatory definition of organic. Each producer could receive a fine for each violation, which means if the producers are not meeting the grazing requirement, their milk will not be classified as organic."

A roar of whooping and hollering went up. After a few minutes, the room buzzed with talk. Caleb patted Thad on the back and raised his voice over the noise. "Hopefully, we will see big results from this action."

A huge wave of relief washed over Thad. "I'm praying that this is the fix for the small dairy farmer."

The noise in the room grew louder with

all the men talking at once. Thad leaned back in his chair and pretended to listen to what others around him were saying.

His mind wandered to his earlier conversation with May. What had he done, sending her away? But he wanted her to make the decision about their marriage based on what both her heart and head wanted, not something forced on her by April's diary or the bishop.

May had to forgive him completely and say so, or it wouldn't work between them. If she couldn't, then he was going to set May free.

He owed her that.

Chapter Twenty-One

May worked for days cleaning the attic, sorting and writing a description for each object and piece of furniture, explaining what it was, whom it belonged to and how old it was. If it had a story behind it, she wrote it down.

Leah would know about her *mamm* and all her *grosseldre*. May was going to tell her how beautiful April had been from the inside out. How her *gut* heart shone and that made her outside glow.

When *Daed* had cancer, April had taken care of him day and night. She'd spent all her time caring for and helping him, or sitting next to him in his room sewing. She'd made rag rugs, quilts, *boppli* blankets, and all kinds of doilies and dresser scarves the *Englisch* loved and had placed them in a consignment shop to help pay the medical bills and the mortgage that had to be taken out against the *haus* for *daed*'s bills.

May wrapped up all the things that April had made. They would make a nice addition for Leah's hope chest when she got married. May wiped away the tears that rolled down her cheek. She regretted her jealousy of April. That was hard for her to admit.

The attic was finally organized and cleaned of years of dust and annoying spiders. Working in the attic had given May plenty of time to think about her life. Maybe Thad was right, and she should visit *Aent* Edna.

On Sunday morning, May checked the church schedule. Preaching was at the

Millers' farm this week. She hitched the buggy and headed off.

At the farm, she glanced around for Janie, didn't see her but found a spot on the bench next to Sarah and Mary. She searched the men's benches on the opposite side of the barn for Thad. Row after row, she scanned faces. Finally, on the last bench, she spotted him, his head down, probably avoiding her. Her heart jumped at the sight of him.

Bishop Yoder's preaching that day was about finding the perfect mate. He said that meant working together for the future, but also working individually, selflessly, to make the other person happy. Only then could a person have the perfect marriage. His message touched May's heart. It was a *gut* recipe for success. He and his *frau* seemed to have a great marriage. His testimony also spoke to her. *Forgive and move on. Don't allow the past to possess you.* Had she done that? Had Thad been right all along?

The bishop ended the service, then glanced from side to side. "I have a *wunderbaar* announcement to make. Janie Conrad and Jonah Hochstetler will be married in four weeks."

Janie and Jonah? Getting married? May hadn't thought Gretchen would ever let that happen. She looked around and found Gretchen. She was staring at May and gave her a smile. May returned the affection. *Ach*, it seemed like Gretchen's heart had truly changed. What a blessing from *Gott*.

On the way to serve the meal, May caught up with her mother-in-law and gave her a hug.

"*Ach*, what was that for, May?"

"You know very well, Gretchen. You and Aaron gave Jonah and Janie your blessing."

"*Jah*, and we gave it to you and Thad, too. Now you two need to make up and quit this foolishness."

May glanced away, then back and nodded. Her mother-in-law was right. And May knew what she had to do.

When she sat for the common meal, she glanced over the tables for Thad, but couldn't find him. She walked into the Millers' *haus* and around the yard, but there was no sign of him anywhere. He must have gone home right after church. She hadn't seen Leah either. Her chest felt as empty as a hollowed-out log.

She helped clean the tables and carried leftovers into the *haus*. Making her good-byes, she hitched her buggy, and urged Gumdrop into a fast trot. Her excitement spurred her all the way home.

Her friends were happy and getting married. And Gretchen was right. She never thought she would be saying that. Now she had to convince Thad that she loved him with all her being.

The next day dawned crisp and bright with only a few clouds puttering across the sky. May hitched Gumdrop. "You have been lazy." She scratched his ears. "You need to get out before it gets too cold. You can sleep all winter, eat oats and get fat until spring."

He shook his head as if he understood her teasing.

She pulled up in front of Bishop Yoder's *haus* and knocked on the door.

Mrs. Yoder answered the door. "*Gut* mornin', dear."

"Morning, Rebecca. Is the bishop in?"

"He's in his office. I'll get him." She swept May with an examining look before she waddled down the hall. There were probably only a handful of reasons most people visited the bishop. *Nein.* Boil that down to two: good news or bad news. Most likely Mrs. Yoder was looking for a hint as to which this was. Amish women liked to spread the news and gossip. May waited by the front door, her hands twisting around in her apron.

After what seemed like an eternity, the bishop finally appeared from a doorway down the hall. "Nice to see you, May. What brings you by?"

"I've need of a *Schtecklimann*—a go-between."

The bishop raised his brow. "Let's go into the kitchen and talk about this over a couple cups of coffee." He closed the front door after May entered.

She took a sip of the strong brew, then added a little of the cream sitting on the table. For the most part, the bishop would know her story. He listened as she talked. When she finished, he chuckled.

May stared at him. "Is this funny to you, Bishop?" Her tart words slipped out.

The bishop reached over and patted May's hand. "*Nein. Nein.* Someday you will look back on this and tell the story to your grandchildren. My advice to you is the same as I give everyone—settle the problem on a buggy ride. You and Thad work all the time. He worries about the dairy farm, you worry about cheese, and you each worry is the other person in *liebe* with me."

May felt heat creep up her neck and burn her cheeks.

"You dwell too much on the past, May. That's why people set the old in the attic. It's past history. We must live in today's world and deal with our present issues. It's okay to go up to the attic and see those old treasures from time to time."

He paused for a moment, his eyes searching her face for a clue to her heart. How did he know she'd been snooping around in the attic?

"The old things were placed there for a reason." He looked at her intently and continued. "Live in the present. Thad is a *wunderbaar* man and he loves you and wants to do right by you. You need to decide what is right for you, then tell him. *Liebe* isn't that complicated. Don't hurt that little *mädel*. She is innocent in all this. Leah loves you unconditionally. You and

Thad are all she has right now, *jah*?" The bishop eyed May.

She knew he wanted an answer but she was fresh out of words.

"I'm always telling folks, go on a buggy ride and get to know each other." He patted her hand. "I'll talk to Thad."

"Just one more thing, Bishop. My *aent* Edna from Shipshewana asked me to come to Indiana and help run her café and bake shop. She gave me three months to make up my mind. The time is up. I called Edna and told her I would take the train Tuesday, the day after tomorrow. I am packed and ready to go, so if Thad wants to see me about our marriage, it will need to be before then."

Before May climbed into the buggy, she gave Gumdrop a few pats on the nose. He raised his head up and down. "*Jah*, you are a smart horse. You knew all along. I think *Gott* whispered in your ear. He probably whispers in mine, too, but I'm too busy talking to listen. What I wanted was right under my nose all this time. Let's stretch your legs."

The bishop's words helped her put her life in prospective. The fall fields were bare and lifeless. They were in a state of restful sleep, a time to replenish strength by letting the natural course of nature wash over the land.

She jerked her head around when Gumdrop turned into the drive. She hadn't even been paying attention; she was home already. The horse passed the *haus* and trotted to the barn. She unhitched and fed Gumdrop, then hurried into the *haus*.

May needed to keep her hands busy and her mind off Thad until it was time to get on the train. Why not start ripping up April's dresses so she could take the strips with her to make rag rugs and save them for Leah.

She was going to miss Leah…and Thad terribly.

Ever since Thad had seen May at church, she kept appearing in his head. Her smoky-gray eyes and auburn hair set a fire in his heart that was hard to put out. Every time he saw her, he wanted to take her in his arms and never let her go.

Gott, *I don't know what you want from me. I felt called to marry April and give her and Leah a chance at a family. Yet the woman I loved and wanted most to have a family with, I alienated.* Gott, *I'm drowning here. I wanted a family with May, and now I'm afraid I've lost her forever.*

Buggy wheels churning the dirt in Jonah's driveway pulled Thad from prayer. He peered out the window. It was Bishop Yoder. Must be important for him to drive all the way out here in the country, and it couldn't wait until Church Sunday.

"Bishop, *gut* to see you. What brings you out here?"

The bishop didn't smile. "Thad, I'd like a few words with you."

He motioned the bishop inside the *haus.* "What's going on?"

"May stopped by to see me. She told me

everything. She said you tricked her into marrying you by leading her to believe there were many complaints about your living arrangements."

Thad's heart almost stuttered to a stop.

"You fibbed to her. *Jah?* You will need to talk to the Lord about that. Do you truly *liebe* May or did you marry her just because Leah needed a nanny?"

The words slammed into Thad's chest. "I regret saying all that. I *liebe* her, and I've done nothing but hurt her. That's why I wanted to make it right by setting her free."

"Thad, she still wants to be your *frau.* You must go talk to her and make it right. But she said to tell you her *Aent* Edna gave her three months to make a decision on whether she was going to move to Shipshewana. She has a train ticket for Indiana for the day after tomorrow, and she will leave if you do not contact her." The bishop looked him squarely in the eye. "You know what you have to do, Thad."

* * *

May heard a buggy come up the drive and peered out the window. It was Ethan, one of the *youngies* who helped do chores.

Her heart felt like a hollowed-out tree stump without Leah and Thad as part of her life. Tears were blurring her vision and she could hardly breathe. As soon as she arrived in Shipshewana, she'd get settled and start to work at the café and stay busy.

She couldn't imagine life without Thad and Leah. The life that she once never wanted, and now she couldn't imagine how she would get along without it.

She waited hour after hour. But Thad didn't come and ask her to stay. Tears welled in her and an ache tore through her heart.

When she heard wheels crunching over the rock in the driveway, she ran to the window. But it was only the SUV that was taking her to the train station. Her throat clogged with emotion as she took one last look around the *haus*.

She told the driver she had luggage, and he said he'd be happy to come into the *haus* and help her.

May walked toward the kitchen door, and stopped. Footfalls sounded coming up the porch. She took a deep breath. A knock sounded loud and firm. The knock of a man who knew what he wanted.

She smiled and slowly opened the door.

Thad stood there holding Leah.

"You didn't have to knock," May said.

"I did, just this once. I needed you to open the door and let me in, not just into your *haus*, but into your heart. I *liebe* you, May. I always have and always will. I know I hurt you by trying to do what was right for someone else. I hope I never have to do something like that ever again."

"*Nein*, Thad. I know why you married April. It took me a long time to come to terms with it, but I promise you, I have. Our belief is that we serve our *Gott* and our community above ourselves. You did what was best for the community, and I wallowed in my own self-pity. I wasn't living our faith. But *Gott* is *gut* and faithful. Marrying you was always my dream and losing you my worst fear come true. I *liebe* you, and now I can live my dream."

She stepped forward. "We both wanted the same thing but worried that the other would say *nein*. You're an honest man. I wouldn't want you any other way. *Ich liebe dich,* I love you, Thad Hochstetler, and always will."

May took Leah from his arms and hugged her tight. Leah smiled and giggled. May shifted her to her left hip. She raised her hand to Thad's cheek and stepped toward him until their lips met for a tender kiss.

He put his arms around May and pulled her and Leah both into a hug. "*Ich liebe dich*, May Hochstetler. We are *ehemann* and *frau* and always will be. And nothing will ever separate us again, for sure and for certain. That's a bargain that I will never be sorry for making."

She stepped back and held up her Amtrak ticket to Shipshewana. "Shall we tear it up?"

Thad paused. "*Nein*, we will give it to the driver, along with his payment."

"When I bought the ticket, an overwhelming fear of losing you came over me. Then I knew what April must have felt like losing Alvin. When I thought about her being pregnant and knowing that she and her *boppli* would be shunned, I realized what she was going through. How desperate her life must have felt like to marry someone whom she didn't *liebe* to give her *boppli* a name. But I'm sure she found some kind of satisfaction in knowing that you, Alvin's *bruder*, was going to marry her, and that you would take care of her and Leah, and raise her like Alvin would have wanted."

She caught her breath. "You asked me a couple of questions a few days ago that I wasn't prepared to answer. But I am now. You asked me if I'd forgotten about the past and that April and you were married. *Nein*, I haven't forgotten, at least not yet, but in time I believe that it will dissolve into the past and become like ashes. It just won't matter, because I tried to put myself in April's situation, and I hope that she would be willing to make the same sacrifice for me. I forgive you, not just because Christ said that if we do not forgive men their sins, our Father in heaven will not forgive our sins, but because we live in community. And I'm glad that you loved your *bruder* enough to marry April and take care of Leah."

He crossed the distance between them and wrapped May in a hug and kissed her tenderly again.

"Me, too, *Daed*. Me, too," Leah called out.

Thad kissed Leah's cheek. "Pumpkin, you will always be part of our hugs."

May wiped the tears from her eyes. "I will always *liebe* you both, and we will always be a family."

Epilogue

"Bishop Yoder!"

May tried to hurry but the bishop could step lively when he had a mind to do it. Perhaps he didn't hear. "Bishop!"

She glanced around at the congregants after preaching to make sure no one else could overhear her request.

She stepped a little faster. "Bishop!"

He stopped and turned around. "May, did you call?"

"Bishop, you seem a little hesitant to talk to me."

"My dear, you and your *ehemann* at times like to stretch the authority of the

Ordnung. I tell you that you can't work outside the home in your cheese factory, so you get the whole community involved so I can't say *nein*. And you organize it during the common meal on Church Sunday. When I wanted to matchmake you and Thad, you resisted. Then when you decided you'd marry him, you two fight and want a divorce." He scowled. "No one I have played matchmaker for has ever had a complaint or asked for a divorce. Just the fact that you even asked for one sets a precedent I don't like. If news of that ever got out, the other bishops would think I have lost control of my community." The bishop whisked out his handkerchief and blotted his forehead. "Now that I got that off my chest, what can I assist you with?"

"Bishop, there are six of us in the cheese factory and one cell phone for the business is just not enough. We would like permission for all of us to carry a phone."

"Certainly not." The bishop waved his hand as if to wave the idea away. "There can be one per business. You will need to designate someone to carry the phone."

"But we all make different kinds of cheeses and have our own orders. For each of us to have a cell phone would be so convenient." She laid a hand on her belly. "And since Thad and I are expecting, he worries about me when I'm away from home."

"And how is your business? Is it all you hoped it would be?"

"It is a blessing, Bishop. It not only pulled us out of debt, but all those who are in it with us have no financial worries. The farm is looking better than ever after all the repairs. And we are thinking about expanding the business and getting on the Iowa Cheese Roundup and getting a star put on the Roundup Map."

"And when is your little one due?"

"In two months."

"So." He rubbed a hand down the breast of his coat. "I have time to think about the additional cell phones."

He turned to walk away, then glanced

back. "*Jah*, I think my matchmaking hat has not lost its credibility. *Gut* day." He turned, raised his hand in the air and waved.

The clip-clop of the horse pulled May's attention to Thad pulling the buggy up next to her and stopping. She stepped up and slid in next to Leah.

Leah tapped the rein against Tidbit's back. "Look, *Mamm*. Get going, Tidbit."

"*Jah*, you are a *gut* driver."

Thad helped Leah sit back in the seat. "Okay, Leah, the horse is trotting so no more tapping. What did the bishop say?"

"He'll think about it. But I'll keep working on him. I think he'll change his mind. I just have a feeling."

"Is that like the feeling you first had about us when we married?"

"*Nein*. After I learned what true forgiveness was, I could trust again and that unlocked the door for us. I asked the Lord to guide my steps, and they led right back to you."

Thad slipped his arm around her, and she slid closer to him. His dark blue eyes locked with hers and stole her heart once again. *"Ich liebe Dich*, I love you, May." He leaned over and gave her a tender kiss.

"Ich liebe Dich, Thad."

"Daed, I want to drive."

Thad raised a brow and glanced at May. "She's taking after you more and more every day."

Peace filled May as she glanced toward Thad with a smile. Her dream had come true. She let her gaze wander to the sky. She had a wonderful *ehemann* and family; who could ask *Gott* for anything more?

* * * * *

If you loved this story, check out
The Amish Baker
by author Marie E. Bast

And be sure to pick up these other
stories of Amish romance

Shelter from the Storm
by Patricia Davids
The Amish Widower's Twins
by Jo Ann Brown
Finding Her Amish Love
by Rebecca Kertz
Courting the Amish Nanny
by Carrie Lighte

Available now from Love Inspired!

Find more great reads at
www.LoveInspired.com

Dear Reader,

Like many small farmers in the Midwest, many Amish farmers are feeling the squeeze from their competitors, the large producers out west. Feeling the pinch, many small farmers have sold out and left the farm.

Thad Hochstetler is a young Amish farmer in Iowa, who banded together with other small Amish farmers to form a cooperative in order to compete and sell their milk to the big chain stores. After losing his wife shortly after childbirth, having a tornado rip through his farm, and the obligation on his mortgage, Thad is overwhelmed with debt.

May Bender's dream had been to marry her beau, Thad Hochstetler, until it turns to dust when he jilted her and married her sister April. After April's death, May helped care for their daughter, Leah, for a year. But with hard feelings still brewing, she decided it was time to move on with her life and relocate to Indiana. That is, until Thad offered her a marriage bargain. Now May is about to discover "that all things work together for good to them that love God" (Romans 8:28).

I love to hear from readers. Tell me what you enjoyed, what inspired you, or your favorite character. Email me at Bast. Marie@yahoo.com, visit me at mariebast. blogspot.com and facebook.com/marie. bast, or mariebastauthor.com, or follow me on Twitter @mariebast1.

Blessings,
Marie E. Bast